Filling the BELLY

Filling the BELLY

TARA MANUEL

THISTLEDOWN PRESS

National Library of Canada Cataloguing in Publication Data

Manuel, Tara, 1973-
Filling the belly / Tara Manuel.

ISBN 1-894345-56-8

I. Title.
PS8576.A575F54 2003   C813'.6   C2003-910397-8
PR9199.4.M35F54 2003

Cover photograph by David Mendelsohn/Masterfile
Cover and book design by J. Forrie
Printed and bound in Canada

Thistledown Press Ltd.
633 Main Street
Saskatoon, Saskatchewan
S7H 0J8
www.thistledown.sk.ca

Thistledown Press gratefully acknowledges the financial assistance of
the Canada Council for the Arts, the Saskatchewan Arts Board, and the
Government of Canada through the Book Publishing Industry
Development Program for its publishing program.

ACKNOWLEDGEMENTS

Special thanks to Ann Rigler for coming out here to hold down the fort.

Special thanks to Janet and David Wall of Devon, England, for the kind use of their flat in Sidmouth, Devon, where the first draft of this novel was written.

Kind thanks to the Tree House Family Resource Centre in Deer Lake, Newfoundland, especially Lilly Ball.

Thanks to my beautiful mother, Janet Manuel, for all her faith and encouragement.

Thanks to my husband, Michael Rigler, who made it possible.

For my husband, Michael Rigler

ॐ

THERE ARE PLACES IN THIS GARDEN where to be is like dreaming with the sun in your belly. The stump where Father sits is one of those places. She leans against him, her leg slung over his knee, and when she breathes, it is the living scent of stories and safe times, of spruce trees and tobacco, of Father with a few jollies in his belly that rumble like thunder when he throws back his head and laughs. He tells her:

"Don't go too deep into the woods during mating season, Rosa my girl."

When he says this he tips his great head toward the river. He has told her these things before. She knows what can happen in the woods. The trees keep her secret. Those black spruce, those red and Norway spruce, the paper birch and the silver. They have wrapped her secret in their bark which seems to tighten and tighten around her belly like a wooden corset. Like a prayer she repeats their names, rhyming them to her memory until she forgets and the words lose their shape, becoming sounds in her head that have no meaning.

> *White, Norway, Black, Red,*
> *Spruce, Spruce, make it dead.*
> *Scots, Stone, Jack Pine,*
> *When I'm old I will drink wine.*
> *River, Yellow, Paper Birch,*
> *I never want to go to church.*

She repeats this prayer until Father begins again.

"The woods are alive. Their memory reaches back into time before men and women and children."

As he talks, he wraps his left arm around her waist. His right hand paws at the ground, ripping rich red brown soil out of the earth and holding it to his nose. He offers her a sniff.

"It all begins with this. This is the creator of life. Don't forget what I tell you," he says.

She chooses to empty her words into the silence of this moment, hoping to pry from him a secret. "Father, why did you set fire to the ski-doo?" When she presses again for a reason he gives her a sip of Blackhorse. Lips inside or around the stubby bottle neck, she never is sure.

From this stump in the garden he will sit to survey his riches; cords and cords of wood, chopped and stacked neatly in rows under tarps drawn tight like the belts around Mother's waist. Behind the stump aways, through the red maple trees, there is a rope upon which to swing. Around and around she keeps Father's black head as a point upon which to focus, allaying the dizziness that can come with spinning. Each revolution is a split second of time when she sees him apart from the world. As he exists in his own right. A man alone with his conscience. His greatness of being seems to fill up his body so that it must stoop a little to show the strain. His eyes are almost as black as his hair and when the sun shines hot in the summer months his chest burns red, deep like the clay in Steady Brook. Her favourite part of him is the gap in his front teeth, stained by coffee and backy, where he'd stuck a nail to flush out a morsel after a meal and a jolly too many. She could not say with words why this part should be her favourite, only that it is a space through which she can see into the inside of him. A crack that might spill out a secret. A split that he might need help mending.

There are enchanted places outside the garden where she loves to wander. Where she and her brothers spend times foraging in thick woods, building and dismantling their rough camps, hiding, seeking, and climbing rocks down the brook to the mouth where they found the dead bullmoose that time, all puffed up, meal for flies, half sunk in the pug. Down by the bog where they hunt for pinfish and tadpoles. Down in the black turf where somewhere dug in deep lies Mother's engagement ring, lost in the time before the paper company flooded the river.

There is the place down by the river where Father ties the boat. Through the trail across the road, slide down the sand cliff grasping stumps and there is the patch of beach. A red sand stage upon which she plays out the death of Mary, Queen of Scots, or the suicide of Juliet, the black and sudden undertow the only witness to these tearful fancies.

Up in Marble Mountain there are places that can heal sorrows. There are old roads, ski trails forgotten for the summer that trace scars in slate and granite over the lumpy back of that ancient hairy lady, marbled footpaths that lead down through woods, tangled knotty woods to the falls, where to swim is to come alive all over again, where being is to understand what God is.

"Rosa, go on in now and do your homework, my brooding girl," he tells her, mussing her hair and pulling the rope up over her head.

"I don't need to do my homework, and anyway, Seamus is waitin to beat the crap out of me for taking his room."

"You tell Seamus I'll break his arms if he touches you. And don't you go provoking him. You've got a sharp tongue, and you've got to learn to control it."

"I've got a smart tongue is what I've got, and don't expect me to go hiding it just because I'm a girl." With hands on her hips she pivots and marches through the garden. She slams the back door, still hearing Father's laughter that begins as a rumble in his belly and erupts through his lungs and throat in a fit of coughing.

In the back porch, the linoleum has cracked to reveal the particleboard beneath. It glares up saucily in its dirty brown dress. Rosa kicks off her rubber boots, and, placing them neatly together, steps over the cracks into the kitchen. The kitchen is a long room, lined with red painted cupboards and counters on one side, with the big fridge and stove, the table and the little black potbellied woodstove on the other. At the front of the room is Father's armchair, his desk for his book, lamp, and ashtray, with Mother's black Windsor chair on the other side, beneath the window. On the table all lined up are twelve loaves of three-bun brown bread, still steaming, with melted butter glistening on each hump, giving the impression of thirty-six little moons.

At the stove Mother stands over an immense pot of mince and doughboys that puff up magically but taste like Cow Brand baking soda. Mother with the far away smile. Mother with the secret life. Mother is beauty. Mother is mystery. There are smells and sounds and gestures that give hints of what she is made of. Yet, only hints, only fleeting moments of insight that leave Rosa yearning to know the secret of this woman. This woman who wears her thoughts on the inside. This woman who believes in God. This woman out of whose eyes light emanates.

After peering around the kitchen to see if Seamus is about, Rosa trots over to where Mother stands and wraps her arms around her from behind. She takes a deep breath, a breath full of Mother's sweet smells; Second Debut, neatly folded clothes, a slightly sweaty animal scent, and shampoo all the way from her hair piled high atop her head. Mother presses her hand.

"Hello, my lovely. How are you today?"

"Where's Seamus?"

"He's out with the boys somewhere."

"Good. Where's the baby?"

"He's sleeping. Why don't you practice your piano while the boys are out?"

"I will later. I've got stuff to do." She runs through the dining room, the living room, through the hall and into her bedroom, slamming the door and fastening the lock. She stands with her back pressed against the door and surveys her empire. Oh joy! Her own room! Word came down on Saturday that Father had decided it was time, and on Sunday, Seamus was uprooted and planted in the room with Jacob so that Rosa, growing girl, could have her own. Of course, Seamus was furious with this new state of affairs and would probably be dirty at her forever. But what could she do? There were so many living in the house and she the only girl. After all, it was only right. Now there would be space for everything, with a lock on the door to keep prying brothers out of private matters.

Rosa sits on her bed, impressing upon her memory this perfection of feeling. Privacy. New freedom. There is much to be done. First, her books must be arranged, according to colours, on the shelves. There are the *Tales*

From the Arabian Nights in hard cover, brown with gold lettering, the *Lives of the Saints* in green paperback, assorted collections of myths, fables, fairy tales, as well as other goodies either given as gifts or found about the house and saved from desecration in the paper walled cities boys would build and destroy. Not to be forgotten are the Nancy Drews that should go on top she thinks, yes, yellow goes best.

There are pages of new words she'd taken down herself from the dictionary. So many words to learn. Words that open windows into other worlds; finer, older worlds, worlds full of magic and mystery. She will place the words on walls, strategically around the room, so that wherever her gaze might fall she will read a new one and its meaning will thus imprint itself upon her memory. There are angry ire and wrath words, sweet mellifluous enraptured words, and wicked nefarious lascivious ones.

After the words will come the lists. These are private and will require a special place to keep them secret should someone enter uninvited. There are lists of *Now*, like the names of plants and flowers Mother divulges lovingly during their walks together. These times are seldom and precious as there is scant allowance for leisure in the running of this household. Rosa's favourites are foxgloves, fireweed, and pitcher plants after rain which look like chalices filled with wine that Father Grace drinks from the altar at Sunday mass. Oh, to taste that wine.

Then there are lists of *Someday*. These include dresses to wear, for like most girls she understands that cutting an attractive figure will just make things easier, and she hopes fervently that one day she will be beautiful. These days, however, she laments the sight of her ever skinned knees, boyish build, and overly freckled face that peers into the mirror gravely communicating its doubt. Since, unlike Seamus, she hasn't been blessed with a talent for drawing, Rosa uses words to describe the kind of garments she hopes one day to wear. Crimson, burgundy, emerald, tawny, ochre, for colours. Taffeta, velvet, damask, silk, linen, and cashmere, for textures. These in shapes that cinch the waist and express the breasts. When, please God, they grow. The ideas for these were gleaned partly from books she had read, half understanding, like the one about Catherine the Great, and partly from ones read easily like Nancy Drews; the ear-marked passages describe crisp cotton dresses, a new one adorned at each twist in the plot.

Very important is the list of places *To Be*. Here is the hope chest of yearning. There are overheard talks in late night from that narrow space behind the living room couch, or from inside the dining room Thing; the top of which pulls out rickety-rick, clack, clack, clack, to hold a myriad plates of food from which Mother serves special dinners. Here, from these hiding places, she hears them telling of times before this house. Times that make her long for a past she never knew. A mythical past when this island was a country and stood alone against the sea.

They remember and they laugh. There was the time when Granny lived in New Brunswick. Well to do Granny who liked her drink and her pills. The older children spent weeks with her during the summers. She would engage the eldest brother Paul, at thirteen, to act as her chauffeur on buying trips over the border to Maine. Propped up on pillows, he'd sit in the driver's seat under the weight of his station's hat, an itchy wool hat she'd ordered from an English magazine, so he'd look the part. Paul had to watch the road through a hole cut out of the newspaper curtain Granny had drawn across the windshield. This curtain was to keep the sun out for the sun made her head ache. Dressed in a floor-length beaver coat in the middle of the summer, she'd sit coolly inside, her body surrounded by the necessary cheap bottles of booze, waving to the border guard. Oh, Good day, Mrs. Keegan! He'd say, letting her pass, and they all laughed. Father pounding the kitchen table with man-sized fist, almost spitting out the cigarette ever pressed between his lips.

There are lands beyond this island, ones heard of and ones imagined, never seen, except in pictures of *National Geographic* and Walt Disney on Sunday nights. Here on the list are named places of which she has heard and read but won't be real until the ground underfoot and the road signs say so. There is the city where Granny now lives, that is Toronto. There is Gramma's land, the land of Mary, Queen of Scots, the land of Scotch currant bun sweating in tin boxes at Christmas. There is Catherine the Great, that is Russia. A cold dream of a country full of peasants with nothing and queens with palaces, jewels, horse-drawn carriages, fur, and lovers, so many lovers. The worst is the place of not knowing in these secluded, surrounded moments of dark night the where and how.

Of life and death importance is the treasure that will own the secret spot in the room. The treasure kept long hidden in the old room shared with Angus and Andrew. The smelly, messy, bunk-bedded room where this treasure was begun after sleepless hours; hiding and writing amidst musty bell-bottoms, holey sweaters, and tattered pictures of smiling white toothed wonders called Donny and Marie Osmond in the ceiling high clothes cupboard of ones who had come before. There are many mildewed corners that hold discards of older ones, the newer ones must keep pushing them back from the centres of rooms to make this house their own.

She has seen photographs, in black and white, of long ago when Mother and Father had come to this house that had three rooms. Then with every year would come a new baby and a new room until there were so many babies that rooms filled up faster than Father could build them. Now it's a long and winding house and the photographs are in colour.

And today this room in which Rosa sits is her very own, in this house, this family, this Newfoundland in the sea. With this room will come new rituals. There will be no more nightly readings by Mother of Dr. Doolittle's adventures, or the caressing of heads by Gramma, toiling and humming over each until sleep comes. No. Now is the time for growing and changing, for new stories and words, for private times. Now she will hide her writings under the grate in the hidden shelf of a heating duct where heat used to come in blasts before Father switched to woodstoves. He said that would save him money and when the power went out he'd still be able to fry up eggs and bacon for supper. And so much better now to wake to the smell of burning bark from the trees that grew across the river. He told her that as long as he only took what they needed to survive the winter, the trees would forgive his cutting.

Now there is privacy to write her words and to hope that somehow through them will be found the secret to long, quiet, restful nights; nights full of sleep and peace. Rosa kneels at the grate that covers the hiding spot, lifts the lid, and reaches into the dank and cobwebbed hole to bring into the light her dearest possession. She pulls back pages of yellowed *Western Star*, peels off the tattered mauve scarf Mother used to wear on her head after her rollers went in and there is the cherished book, a plain black cover, hard and big, only half-filled with her nocturnal scribbles. She opens to the last page, and moving her finger along the lines, reads silently, lips moving to shape the words too private to be spoken aloud.

When my dreams are so disturbing that they wake me up, I get out of my bed and hide here in this mouldy closet. I take my flashlight from way down beneath my blankets and climb in here to find my secret book and pen. Everyone else sleeps, but I am awake and writing. This is bad what I do, but I cannot stop myself. Prayers will not make my dreams go away. God does not comfort me, he does not know me, does not care to grant me peace, even after I have prayed for so long that I may sleep. This is why I suspect he is a lie. There are many other reasons, but my dreams are the best one. If God gave a damn, he'd let me sleep.

Tonight I dreamt of the woods again. I don't understand why I am so afraid. I love the woods, but I am afraid of them. Why do I fear what I love? I was climbing Marble Mountain, through the trees, the higher and deeper I got, the less control I had over my fear. What I was looking for is the footpaths that are so familiar to me, yet I could not find them. I could not find them and I was stumbling through the woods in the dark. The branches scratched their brittle names into my body, telling me I belong to them. I was so deep in the woods that I knew there was no way out in the dark. No way out of the dark. I was wet with panic that seeped into my insides like water through walls in the spring. I heard a rutting moose snorting at me from behind and I was off again, crashing through the trees. A grouse exploded out of the brush in front of me and I screamed. I covered my face with my arms, still running from the moose, still stumbling, clawing my way through the trees. I felt the stinging of a hundred slashes on my body and hands. I really felt it. I was screaming and crashing through the woods, still hearing the savage breathing of the moose, still feeling the wings of the grouse beating against my arms, when suddenly

I found myself standing at the edge of a pond. For a moment I was filled with happiness to be at the water standing under a clear sky. There were no dangers. I will sleep here at the edge of the water I thought. I lay down, there was moss beneath me and the air was so warm I knew I wouldn't miss my blankets. I tried to sleep but couldn't because of the fire that burned on the other side of the water. I sat up, and as I stared I realized it was our garden I was seeing and at the back of the garden a fire burned. The longer I looked, the more I saw in the fire. Now I know what it was. The ski-do was burning. And Father was there. If only in silhouette, he was there. And he wouldn't do anything about it. And I don't know why. My dreams make me feel so tired.

Rosa closes the book and places it on her lap. Her back is tense and hunched, her neck disappearing between her shoulders. From this place on the floor, she can see just over the window sill the entrance to the trail. Now there begins to play in her mind a memory. As if a film has been turned on in her head that she cannot control she watches, both enthralled and terrified by the images, her body frozen in position. Now in her mind she walks into the trail. Without looking, she knows the line of every tree that surrounds her. Wet, rotting leaves blanket the ground. Sodden sticks crackle under her feet. She comes to the place where the maple bow bends across the way. The trusty battered bough. Bent from years of children sliding on its back. Here past the yellow pebbles she turns to the right. There in front is the mound at the base of the old oak tree. She lies on her belly over the mangled roots. Over the seat of shame. She presses her cheek to the cold earth. She closes her eyes.

ཨཨཨ

In the dank place in her memory the sun shines. It is unusually hot for a Labour Day weekend. Children's laughter tickles the breeze. The lower road is cluttered with large machinery. Tractors, digging machines, and paving tanks. This is the last year of the floods. They are raising the road up to prevent further damage. Much to the children's dismay. The unguarded machinery has become a playground for the kids who live by the river. They climb over and around the roller and dump truck, pretending to operate them, pretending to work.

"Anyone who wants a kiss follow me into the trail!" shouts the boy with the freckles. The boy with the bad temper. The boy who fascinates. She follows. Alone. Far behind she clings to the branches that line the trail. Picking leaves, she rubs them back and forth between her fingertips until the green juice wets her hands. She must follow. She reaches the old oak tree and stands listening for him. Her stomach flutters and she decides to go back to the road, back down by the machines where her brothers are. As she turns, the freckled boy grabs her by the back of the neck and thrusts her to the ground. Her cheekbone smacks off a twisted root and her wind is taken. His grubby hand presses the back of her head, shoving her face into the earth. She opens her mouth to cry out, but he pushes harder, rank leaves filling the space where sound wants to be. She is choking now as his other hand tears her pants down at the back. The elastic waist scrapes her skin as her body racks in a silent scream. She is being torn apart from the bottom up. Piercing her flesh in that private place. Her skin down there is splitting, ripping, cracking open and the pain is screaming inside her at a deafening pitch, making her mad and madder until all she can do is to stop the sound. She smacks her head on the thick root, its bark peeling back like sunburned skin. The screaming inside her grows louder and louder as she smacks and smacks, her head thudding against the root as blood pours from her nose and the holes she is digging in her forehead. Smack. Smack. Smack. Smack. Smack.

ৡৡৡ

With a quick direct motion, she reaches her hand into the duct and pulls from the unseen shelf a white tube. Struggling to control her shaking hands, she unscrews the top of a tube of toothpaste and throws back her head to squeeze the stuff in and swallow. She replaces the tube and the book in the hole, then puts the grate back in its place. On her hands and knees she sways back and forth, waiting for the cool peppermint feeling in her belly, a numbing feeling. Why she does this she knows not. She makes promises to herself to give up these habits, but they do have some value. She needs them to stop her from thinking. To turn off her memory.

"Ah — R-r-r-rosa!" he roars, interrupting her swaying. Rosa is quiet, waiting for him to continue. He clears his throat, lingering outside the locked door. She waits for the inevitable second throat clearing before responding. This is Jacob, who never enters without invitation, the special brother who is the heart of this home.

"Come on in, Jake buddy!"

"Ah R-r-r-rosa, the door is locked!"

Rosa hops up to open it, and feeling a little sick, goes and sits on the bed.

"Come on in for a chat, Jake. Close the door, too."

"Yup, 'cause now's not the time to do a — " giggles Jacob, encouraging Rosa to fill in the blank.

"Poo," whispers Rosa. This is just the naughty answer he was waiting for. He giggles especially at dirty rhymes. He's the rhyming man. Always ready to echo your words with a rhyme, sensible or not. That's not the point.

Jacob stands in the centre, belly protruding beneath his belt, his good hand buried in the pocket of ruddy brown corduroys, the other little one tucked in at his side, fingers curling back toward his wrist, as if his arm cradles a wounded bird. He stands, taking it all in, meets Rosa's eyes, and both burst into giggles.

"Lay me five, Jake," and he does so hard their hands meet with a thwack. "Have a seat, buddy."

"Wouldn't want to be putty!" Jacob aligns himself with the edge of the bed, then drops and bounces.

"S-S-S-S-So Ah R-r-r-rosa."

"Yah, Jake?"

"How's the new room, pretty cool, eh?"

"Yes, my love, it's pretty cool all right." Rosa pats his back. Another pause.

"Hey Rosa."

"Hey Jake."

"Ya, hay is for horses. Didja know that?" Jake slaps his knee and breaks into a laugh that is pitched so high it makes the skin inside her ears sting.

Jacob is a subject that inspires passion. He endures much teasing from siblings, however, there is no allowance of such from anyone outside the family. Any unfortunate soul who ventures thus will be met with threats and worse; poundings from more than one of the Keegans. The pride the family takes in Jacob can ruffle feathers and cause tempers to fly savage.

Jacob delivers *The Western Star* newspaper to all the homes in Steady Brook. In summer on his three-wheeled bicycle, given him by All Hallows School, he careens at speeds too painful to watch as the ride might end in a crash, bloody road burns, and a bruised ego. In winter he delivers on foot through snow so laborious he arrives home blue from the cold, late into dark, his supper overdone and waiting in a great heap on a plate in the oven. If there is money to be made, Jacob will make it. He always has money. He'll lend it, too, if you don't mind spending the hour or so it takes to convince him to part with it. Jacob is the stalwart of community, keeper of names and incidental facts, charmer of women and all who take time to wait for words around pauses.

Rosa grins at him, "Mary Brown's got the best legs in town."

Turning his face away and suppressing a laugh only long enough to force the words out, he says, "Yah, 'cause they're open 'til two AM."

They both laugh at this joke that is as old as the fried chicken joint itself. Still giggling in a way that manifests itself as hisses and spurts, Jacob as always adds, "Don't tell Mom I said it 'cause she hates that one."

Rosa throws her arms about him to make her promise. He returns the hug with such strength, his rounded wrist digs a pit in the small of her back. Sometimes he will inspire in her an almost painful affection, it is the way he will look sometimes, so fragile, so innocent, so unchanging that to behold him is to behold goodness incarnate, but goodness that is not aware of itself, which makes it open to harm.

The call to supper rings out and Rosa and Jacob join the stampede to the kitchen. Gramma dishes the food onto plates. Sweet Scottish Gramma, with eyes as blue as the bay on a cold, sunny day, the infinite gray braid wound round her head, skin of lily-white blushing pink and pinker like the dreamy chalk of Edinburgh rock she would bring home from rare trips overseas.

"I'm first!" yells Seamus, stamping on Rosa's foot as he lunges for the full plate in Gramma's hand. Rosa punches him hard in the back and sends him flying into Gramma, immediately regretting having done it. The plate lands on the floor and breaks, and suddenly everybody is yelling. Seamus grabs Rosa's forearm and applies his deadly Indian sunburn, wrenching the skin in opposite directions. Rosa uses her free hand to pull his hair, the black curls threatening to detach themselves from his scalp. Seamus screams and calls her that name no one will hear again after leaving this place.

"Diarrhea Dog!"

Mother and Angus jump in between, prying them apart.

"Stop it! Stop it! Stop it!" Mother cries and takes over the serving of the meal, too disheartened to carry out an investigation into the cause of the outburst.

"Oh, for goodness sake, I wish ye'd behave in a civilized fashion!" Gramma bends to clean up the mess. "And such a waste of food. Such a blasted waste of good food."

Mother dishes out supper to each so that by the time she gets to sit down, half of the family have finished and the cacophony of after meal has begun. Father will come in for his when the young ones have been fed and he can enjoy a little peace.

After supper comes piano practice. First, the monotonous scales, more complicated each week since lessons began with Gunter Goodrich. Better to learn them well and not make him pretend to be angry since he smells so good, dresses like a prince, and buys them both cream crullers and hot chocolate from Tim Hortons. Sometimes he gives Mother back the money paid monthly for lessons. These kindnesses burn. Money is tight, she knows this, she understands that adding up pennies at the grocery store means, "times is hard b'ye."

After scales comes the best part. Bach's *Invention Number One*, or the *Prelude* she has just mastered. Simple clean notes over and over, her pleasure does not diminish with repetition. Tonight the sherry flows and Gramma sits down to play "The Keel Row", and other Scottish melodies she improvises. All the while her feet mark the steps of the Highland Fling. Tonight is lucky, for Mother takes her turn, perching her glass of wine on the milk-spotted mahogany of this precious piano gift from Gramma and Granda.

"My love, sing 'Drink to Me Only'," Father calls out from his seat in the kitchen. Tonight, times are good. He grows misty as she sings. Her voice feathers down, a pillow to dream of woman's body and mind, when the time will come to leave this island far behind, and to know what other lands exist beyond the sea.

"Rosa it's time for bed now," says Mother, bending down to kiss Rosa, sunk in her chair.

"My precious pink rosebud." These words Rosa loves to hear.

Sitting in bed, her back pressed against the headboard, Rosa reads *The Bike Tour Mystery*, and waits to see the glow from Gramma's bedroom light extinguish in the snow. This is a new game between them. A point of pride. The fastest reader wins. Gramma is caught up in the whirlwind that is Nancy Drew's life. Her room is next to Rosa's, both have windows that look out on the front garden where lives the crabapple and the Scotch pine trees. Rosa waits until the trees are dark and Gramma's ears are sure to be closed to all but dreams. The she gets out of bed, takes her towel and book, and creeps into the bathroom.

Quiet night signals time for rituals to begin. These are baths in rare hot water from the tank in the kitchen cupboard closet which stores, on raw two-by-four shelves, sunlight soap, long bars cut as needed. Maybe this is the secret of Father's silky hair. Night is the only time when water runs hot enough to fill the milk green tub in the new bathroom on the hall side of the house, and no brother will bang his fist on the door to enter.

ৰ

AGAIN I AM AWAKE when I should be sleeping. By the red lights on my clock I see that it is seven past three in the morning. By the red lights on my clock I see that I am still in my new room, but I am not really in my room. I look through the window and beyond the trees I see the entrance to the trail, and that is where I am. I am inside the trail and I am remembering what I wish I could forget. Too often I lose control of my thoughts and they lead me back down into these murky, dank places where being makes me want to punch myself in the face until I bleed from my eyes 'til they are blind. If I could not see then maybe I would be unable to leave my room at night when I should be sleeping. How I wish I were sleeping.

When I turn out the light at night, I lie inside my covers, and close my eyes. I imagine clean, beautiful places, like the top of Marble Mountain, like Lark Harbour Park, like Cow Head. I imagine lying in a field of red clover, picture the insides of blueberries, taste the water at the top of the falls. After a time I feel myself beginning to slip into sleep and I think, Great! this will be wonderful, and it is, for a few hours. And then it begins to happen. It's this horrible feeling in my belly. It's like a big hole. And I don't mean hunger. My belly is the centre of my body. It's where I feel everything. Love and precious stories and warmth and happiness I always felt lived in there. And when I put my hands on it that feeling of everything being good and right would spread throughout my whole body and flow from me out to everybody around me. And it was me that was good. But I'm not anymore. I'm ruined. I'm dirty. And now all that good is gone through the hole. And it's always at night that I feel it most. I am sleeping when suddenly I become aware of sweating, sitting bolt upright, and my mind having left the house. And my mind torments me with things I want to forget. Things I can't bear to name. And it's the hole in my belly that wakes me, that keeps me from sleeping, from feeling good. I know when it happened and I can't tell anyone.

ঔঔঔ

Rosa wakes. She opens one eye, squinting as a hint of daylight spills through the doubled glass, onto the sill, over the scratched false marble headboard, puddling the half of her freckled face that peeks out from under peach sheets. Rap, rap, soft, white knuckled rapping at the door.

"Rosa! Rosa! It's time to get up now. It's seven o'three already. There's no time for dilly-dallying this morning, you've got to catch the bus." This is the usual, in three to five minute intervals, on school mornings. When Gramma speaks her name, the r's rolling softly off her tongue like syrup from a spoon, it makes her smile.

"I'm up. I'm up, Gramma," comes assurance from between her half-closed lips. She sits up, and drawing the curtain, stares out the window. Everything seems so innocuous in the morning. What's there to fear from that old oak tree in there? The big one, half rotted, standing like a dying sentry at the forking of the trail. The tree that won't let her forget. The tree whose roots are gnarled, digging into her belly like a bed of new bones.

Again comes the rapping, Gramma has grown impatient.

"Rosa, it's now almost ten past, will yea come on out!"

"Yes, Gramma, I'm coming now!" again from lips that will not open fully until after "Hi, Hi's," and cuddles from Father's warm lap. Then hugs from Mother, who, busy with morning, will indulge until her mouth opens, ready for food. And what food awaits. This home restaurant of a kitchen serves up feasts of blood pudding, eggs omleted, fried, boiled, or scrambled, with bacon crisp or fatty, French toast on brown, white, or raisin that Mother bakes in alternating batches during the week. She makes whatever is required to quell appetites and send little ones on time to school.

Time for the frigid morning walk in half dark amongst Keegans spilling out of the house and up the road. Past the house where that freckled boy used to live before they moved to Labrador. Eyes straight ahead. Think of something else. Past the dark house on the corner by the river, the house that can't be seen for the trees lining the land, the one with the savage dog who barks, speeding young ones on their way. Now the inevitable sprint from the riverbend when they see the bus pulling into stop. Old Buck will wait, his waxed handlebar mustache twitching with impatience. He isn't so bad really, even though he grunts a little when you're late. Occasionally, if someone is unruly, he'll stop the bus and make them walk home. Like her older brother, Matthew. One of the times he mouthed off, Buck stopped on the highway by the place where squatters live on the hill, kicked him out and drove away. That was before Matthew left home. He left a long time ago to live in Toronto. He always had to fight. It is embarrassing to remember being pinned to the floor as he encouraged the dog to lick her face, its tongue lapping inside her mouth while he called her that name no one will hear again after leaving this place.

On the bus are kids who live in subdivision houses, plastic, new, and ones who live down by old riverbank Humber, or along dirt roads by the brook. Two of these are Don and Ronnie Gosse. They're good for a laugh, especially since last summer when, seduced by Father's tales of the Baloney Bogs, a wondrous place where wild baloneys lived and could be hunted, they woke their parents before five in the morning begging them to pack their lunches because Mr. Keegan had promised them a journey aboard a ship powered by the machine with curved blades that churns earth in the potato garden, and they believed he would take them. Sweet Father having jolly time on his stump by the wood pile, holding court, telling tall tales to the neighbourhood children. Tales of fantastical places and creatures. Tales of the Great Albino moose he saw once as a boy. Tales with high adventure and happy endings.

The bus pulls into All Hallows, overlooking the bay. School isn't so bad, except for the days when all children must cross the road to the church to go to confession in the light room. In this room you must kneel before the priest and tell all your sins so that he may forgive them. Bless me Father for I have sinned. I am a child. I am a girl. I am guilty. Take away my shame.

In Newfoundland Culture class, the teacher asks: "How many of you consider yourselves to be Newfound-landers?" Hands go up all around. "How many of you consider yourselves to be Canadian?" Rosa realizes with horror that hers is the only hand raised as others look on with reproach. "There's more than this island," she justifies silently. She knows that beyond the confines of these rugged shores the world is happening in other tongues in other lands, and she wants to think herself a part of all that.

At school she speaks in the way she imagines is the proper way, over enunciating, employing words from her pages as often as possible, trying not to sound like a Newfoundlander. She walks with her head too high in the air, and is welcomed by cold shoulders, sometimes hissing from girls who say nasty things behind backs. "This is just the way I am," Rosa intones to herself during those walks down corridors when thirty seconds can last an hour.

The school is large and old, with ceilings so high an Indian rubber ball can't even bounce up to touch them. All rooms on the bay side have great walls of windows from which harbour porpoise can sometimes be seen if the sulfur from the paper mill doesn't cloud out the day. That rotten egg stink is so bad, even shutting the windows can't keep it out. This city is all wrong. There is no free place for climbing rocks down to the water that becomes sea. Corner Brook is too much mill, too much raw sewage sullying what should be a place of beauty. Steady Brook is so much better since smells are trees and water is for swimming on sunny afternoons on Sandy Beach. To get there you have to go through the trail, down the sand cliff to the river and along, ducking under branches. Father can swim the whole way across with a run, dive, and back again. Rosa wishes she was old enough to stand on the sunken Pepsi machine several meters off shore and wave back to everyone.

After school they will make their way home in twos and threes, kicking through leaves that carpet the ground in hues of rust and gold, under a darkening sky, the air perfumed with winter's imminence.

"Rosa, you got a quarter?" Angus asks, the sound whistling through front space where teeth had been.

"I only have fifty for myself. What happened to your tooth fairy money?"

"Thas gone long ago. Come on b'ye just twenty-five cents!"

"All right, but you'd better pay me back next allowance," says Rosa, reluctantly handing it over. She pushes open the heavy wooden door, and stomps the snow off her boots before entering the store. Bertha Hardy has a name that Rosa likes to call out loud. Bu-urr-thaaa. Like a cross between a brass instrument and a whiskey jack. They will often giggle about the time older brother Mark sent Jacob up to get some elbow grease. In good faith she called the house to offer turtle wax instead, her sweet shrill voice chirping down the line.

"Fifteen Swedish berries, five bananas, two strawberries, and one more berry please, Mrs. Hardy," says Rosa, suppressing a desire to give her interpretation of the woman's first name. Angus buys a jumbo Mr. Freezie.

The two trudge down the road, stopping to read the large painted signs just placed in the yard where the new Pentecostals live.

"Seek the lord and yea shall live!" Angus bellows in a voice that belies his size and years.

"Repent yea of thy sins and the gates of heaven shall be opened unto thee!" Rosa adds, loving the freedom of hollering. They look at one another and crack up.

"I loves soul preaching!" exclaims Angus.

"You're good at it," she says and they begin again, competing for the loudest and the most outrageously pious, stopping down at the boom to munch their treats and look out over the water.

"Whirley Anstey's building a camp over there. Jen's helping him, too. She's some strong for a girl. He got a barge built to cut through the ice when it gets bad."

Angus is the closest in age to Rosa, and soon will be too big to pick fights with, she laments, running her mitted hand over his blond curls. He jerks away. They stand for a moment, watching the first snow of the season fall. The branches on the far shore use the snow as yarn, and ever so slowly they will knit themselves a new coat.

"I LOVES NEWFOUNDLAND!" shouts Angus in a not uncommon fit of passion.

"So do I," agrees Rosa, "but I'm getting out of here," she promises herself, kindling the fire smoldering in someday. She stares out over the swift black Humber, letting her eyes go soft, letting the edges of sight blur. In her mind she slips out of her coat and shoes and steps into the cold black water. The black bark tree skin from all the years the paper company sent forests downstream to Corner Brook, to the edge of the bay, to where salt water meets fresh, pricks at the soles of her feet. There is many a tree that went to its grave down here, out past the shore where the bottom drops away and the currents run hard and deep. The salmon have all gone now, having fought their way through the open sea, through the draggers and sharks, the Bay of Islands, the poison mouth of Corner Brook harbour. Through a thousand hooks on Angler's lines, through illegal nets, through impossible odds to find their way home to the upper Humber, to rest and lay their eggs. Silver skinned, sharp nosed, whip backed, they are the warriors come home once again. Rosa listens hard for their stories of far away lands, of foreign waters and fish, but the Humber is silent. The surface black and still belies its true nature, its true force. Lose your footing little girl, take one step too far and you will be swept away forever, and Father won't save you. Father won't be there to save you.

ৡৡৡ

At home Mother stands over the stove, the steam from a boiling beef tongue glistening on her skin. That skin from another world. Skin ripe like an olive rubbed in its own oil. Like the ones Father'd brought from Kensington Market when he went to visit Granny last year. But something about Mother seems different. And something will never be the same.

ৡৡৡ

This night does not bring sleep. This night she writhes in her bed like a storm tossed ship.

Too tired to read, and too awake to sleep, she throws back the covers and puts on her dressing gown. She goes into the hall, passing slowly through the dark. Wood splinters prick her bare feet. In the living room, light from the street lamp slides in, casting long plant shadows from the sill to the floor. Floral ghosts. She passes over them, watering each with an invisible watering can, speaking silent words of reassurance to each as she goes. From the dining room she hears the click-click of knitting needles, and passing into the kitchen, discovers her Mother sitting in the Windsor chair, knitting furiously by candlelight.

She stands for a time, regarding her in this descriptive light. She wonders if this is her secret custom. Turned in on herself, she is so focused on the wool in her hands that she does not notice her daughter. The knitting is so fast that the garment seems to grow before Rosa's eyes. The wool is a dark boreal green, her mother's favourite colour. Everything she knits is green. Mother says there are so many shades of green that one could knit enough to cover the earth without ever having to use another colour. Maybe this is why she knits instead of sleeping.

Her dark hair, loose from the customary bun now falls about her face, over her broad sharp shoulders, and reaches almost to her waist. Her brow is furrowed, concentrated on her work, but there is something else. Something not the same.

Suddenly she drops her knitting, and covering her face with her hands, begins to weep, the muffled sounds heaving out of her like the twisted agony of an injured animal. Rosa stands awkwardly in the dark, guilty at having witnessed her mother's private anguish, and wanting to give comfort. Mother looks up.

"Rosa, my darling, what are you doing up?" she asks, her voice high and fragile.

"I can't sleep."

"No? Nor can I."

They regard one another for a moment. Rosa goes to her, removes the wool and needles from her lap, places them carefully on the black desk, and wraps her arms around her.

"Whatever happens you must know we love you. Your father and I love you all." Her cryptic tone is unsettling. What is wrong? Rosa wants to ask, but is afraid to speak directly. She plucks up her courage.

"Mom, why are you crying?"

Mother takes a deep breath.

"It's nothing for you to worry about my darling. We must ask God to look after us all. We must pray for the courage to overcome our fears. He will look after us."

These words meant as comfort have the opposite effect. Something must be terribly wrong if only God can help. Through the dark cracks the sound of Father coughing. Rosa covers her ears. The two stare silently at one another while the horrible sounds go on and on.

"I hate it when he does that!" Rosa spits, surprised at her vehemence.

"He can't help it. He can't help it," Mother says, shaking her head from side to side. As they hold one another in the candlelight the coughing rumbles on; deep, wracking, compulsive.

"Go back to bed, Rosa, I must go in to him now." She gives her a little nudge on the bottom, gets up and fills a glass with water at the sink, and hurries into the bedroom.

Unable to listen to him any longer, Rosa runs into her room. She closes the door and goes to the grate. She lifts it and reaches down into the hole. Coming up with a box of matches she puts the grate back in its place and gets into bed, pulling the matches out one by one and chewing the tops off of each, swallowing the salty, gritty stuff, and digging the blunt ends into her gums. Tasting blood in her mouth, she begins to weep. Weeping for the unknown thing that is very wrong in this house. Weeping because she made her gums bleed, weeping because she is so tired her hands are shaking. She sleeps. She dreams. She wakes.

ৡৡৡ

I was dreaming of stepping out of the house in a brown leather coat trimmed around the neck with rabbit fur, soft with autumn fur and I was struttin' in my struttin' coat all over Steady Brook. I wore that leather like a coat of armour and I was fast and sleek, a maiden for all time, a giantess in my own mind. Nobody else knew I was there.

I headed up the tracks in the dark between the frozen bulrushes and the scraggly spruce until I reached the trail. It was black, far from the lights, and the moon was an orange crescent in an azure sky. I crossed my arms in front of me and passed through the trees, my feet finding the trail leading to the Tarzan tree. It is an old paper birch, with a shipping rope tied to the swinging branch, the one that extends out over a ravine, the water lying way way down where the saltwater rabbits are. I gripped the rope, stepped backwards as far as it would reach, then ran to the edge and jumped. For a long moment I was flying. The moon over the Humber river whispered to the back of my head like my mother's hand and I was a happy flying child. The twisted alders on the far shore beckoned to me like benevolent wizards. I swung out over the river, far across to the other side, let go the rope and fell. The alders held up their branches and when they caught me my head filled up giddy with their beautiful perfume. How I love that smell.

And then it happened again and all the sweetness of that dream fell out through the hole and the next thing I knew I was lying in a snowbank, mute with terror. What there was to fear I could not name. The worst has already happened to me. Hasn't it? I stood up, and brushing the snow from my clothes, began to walk towards the house, all the time imagining dark things slashing out at my ankles. Running up my pant legs. Crawling into my belly.

It was cold and dark and I was afraid to enter the house. I was afraid that if I opened the door, everything would be changed and I do not want change. I stood under the winter sky strong with wood smoke from a valley of spruce and birch trees and prayed that I wouldn't wake until the morning, that I would find myself in my own bed, in my own house, hearing the rowdy thumping of a crowd of Keegans.

ॐ

TODAY IS SUNDAY, always a somber day, as if her body knows inherently the dawn of the Sabbath as the day to indulge the spirits. They must all get up early for compulsory ten thirty trips to mass. Mass begins later for the Keegans as they never arrive on time. They will all pile, cranky and complaining, brothers half-cleaned and sloppily dressed, into the old green Granada that is falling apart.

Father is a big man. When he gets into the car he pushes back against the seat so that now the upright part of the driver's side lies flaccidly against the one behind it and cannot be adjusted to support a smaller person. This means that when Mother drives, like on Sundays as Father never goes to mass, Rosa must sit in the back behind her with her legs up against the back of the driver's seat, knees locked to hold Mother in place. The passenger's side door does not open, the window does not close. Everyone must enter and exit through the driver's door which will not close on its own and is held in place by a rigging rope tied round the top of the window frame and looping across the front seat.

Occasionally, the knot will not be untied, and everyone has to crawl out of the passenger's window, Gramma going first. Once, while racing through Humbermouth over butterfly bumps that Rosa loves because of the feeling they make in her belly, the rope came untied, the door swung open, and it almost hit two old ladies who were chatting along the side of the road.

Mother always races to mass, surpassing the speed limit. She cruises on the way home so that she may enjoy the scenery, nod to the man in the mountain, and reflect on the homily. During these languorous drives, idle tempers will often rise to the point of insanity. Usually there are nasty shouts, fist fights, and tears in the back seat. The trips to mass seem to be timed so that they arrive just in time for the Gospel, a great line of them, led by Mother with her head held high, marching past the observant congregation, up to the front pew that is always left empty. Father Grace will stop, nod, and wait for them to settle before resuming the service. Gramma says that as long as they arrive in time for the Gospel, God will understand, and they'll be worthy of receiving Holy Communion. What is the measure of worthiness?

Rosa's embarrassment at this parade is so great that she is often overcome with uncontrollable giggles which spread like a virus to the boys. They bloom into full bellied guffaws during the communion hymn when Jacob throws back his head and sings with tremendous passion in a falsetto that is rarely, if ever, in tune, and can overpower the whole congregation. When re-entering Steady Brook, Rosa ducks down in the seat, anxious that no one should see her riding in this old bomb of a car. Yes, today is *Sunday*.

After the usual business, on the way home from mass, round the riverbend by Shelburne island where there is said to be pirates treasure, Mother says, "You must all gather in the kitchen, for your Father has something to tell."

She says this in a practiced off-hand way, as if she has decided that it is the best tone to use for such a request. A formal family meeting. A first.

Rosa silently lists all her recent actions that might solicit Father's disapproval. Surely there is nothing he could know about, let alone call a meeting about? There is that feeling of guilt which cannot be washed away, like being born with an invisible second sin that grows as she grows, dreams as she dreams, wakes as she wakes.

In the kitchen she sits on one of the sturdy old oak chairs, her back warmed by the woodstove, covered with orange peels from morning laid out to dry on top. Brothers gather round. Mother and Gramma, too, their faces creased with worry lines. What is wrong? There hasn't been much to overhear lately in the hours after dark. And here sits Father, not out cutting as is customary on a weekend, but sitting with a jolly, and so early in the afternoon.

"I have something to tell you," he addresses his audience of different sizes. Rosa looks down to attend to her thumb nail, greened with wax scraped from the seat of her chair.

"I've been for tests at the hospital, and we heard yesterday from Dr. MacLaren."

How strange it is that this family should be gathered so together in silence. Rosa tries to remember a time like this and can't.

"I have been diagnosed with lung cancer and given about six months to live, maybe longer if the treatment takes and the cancer goes into remission."

There is quiet. With her hands spread on the table before her, Rosa feels the slick of a calendar. She takes a sudden interest in antique model cars, one for each month, and she wonders how fast they go and who can afford to buy?

"What's *submission?*" asks Angus, breaking the silence.

"Remission is the word," sighs Father, hauling long on his cigarette. "It means if the treatment kills the cancer cells, I may live longer."

Oh. How long?

"How long for?" asks Seamus.

"I don't know."

Oh. There must be something finer to think about. Rosa closes her eyes and concentrates on the pungent citrus scent wafting from behind. Mother stands with her hand on Father's shoulder, working at a smile hidden behind tears and a runny nose, pulling out a tissue ever found tucked in the sleeve of her blouse.

"Of course I don't know how things will go. I may be able to work through the year but regardless of that, some things will have to change."

Rosa finds the cars ever more engaging and can't look up from February's model. Red and chrome, wheels black rubber, silver spokes crossing in kaleidoscopic lines, things will change? What things? Not Grand Lake, she hopes fervently. In Grand Lake lives the log camp Father built in the time even before the older ones were born. All logs, chinked with moss. One room with two huge mattresses hiked up on stumps to support their reckless fun. Mother cooks meals atop the little Coleman stove that emits a gassy smell. They eat meals at the picnic table with the plastic cover, overlooking the window where they once watched flies eating a great dump Angus had so saucily taken on the ground, and laughter ran wild.

To get there takes a bumpy nine-mile ride down a dirt road in Pasadena. Then two hours across the lake in the aluminum boat adorned in faded stripes of purple, white, and blue. Over waves so fierce you must keep your mouth shut to prevent your stomach from hurling out. Father sits atop his tool box, flush with the arse of the boat, roaring like a bullmoose. Rosa always worries he will be seized backward by the violent waves claiming him for their own. Yet never does he falter, one hand on the handle steering, the other pinching a cigarette, ashes flying into spume.

There in the camp, where bedtime isn't a set hour, Father will tell stories of the Great Albino moose he saw once around these parts, long ago. There are only four on the whole island of Newfoundland, he says, and they have the gift of speech.

"What did he say?"

"That I must repeat to no one."

Rosa will roll her eyes when he goes on about the Albino moose. He gets a kick out of telling them tall tales. Still, she creeps out to the number 19, for so it is named, to go pee, shoulderchecking all the way for the white moose of secrets. Opening the lid, she fears the creatures that may overcome the lime and rise to bite. These fears grow worse during the long walk back to camp over roots, moss, and things that have no name.

"Sure you know not so long ago all the houses in Newfoundland had outhouses," Mother will say to assuage her indignation at this inconvenience. This is no comfort. Rosa has read of women written about in books that have chamber pots fashioned out of gold and silver to be emptied by servants. She desires no less.

In the morning she will peek, bacon in mouth, over the stoop to the sight of Father's bare arse rising out of the frigid water like a great white whale. Rosa waits to bathe in Dragonfly brook, where they take the boat after breakfast, anchoring at Glover island. The brook was named by Mother for the beasts in magnificently coloured bodies with wings that stretch out like fantastical eyelashes. They meet in profusion at this haven of pale green water over bleached white rocks separated by lines of algae in provinces, like the map of Canada.

Rosa sits, eyes riveted on February's model, her mouth hanging open, a puddle of drool wetting the glossy page, turning it matte. The children furtively regard Father, looking for physical signs of his weakness. The silence is broken by a grilled cheese sandwich frying in the pan. Everyone busies themselves with eating and one-by-one, hugs and I love you's with Father. A sharp punch to the upper arm breaks her trance.

"What's wrong with you, my dear? Go and give your Father a hug b'ye."

Rosa whips her head up to look at the offending brother and kicks him hard in the groin. Seamus buckles over, sinking his teeth into Rosa's thigh on the way down. She screams, and with both hands grips this unfortunate's thick curls and pulls with all her might, screaming again when she sees blood and skin on the black clumps of hair staining her palms. Seamus turns and charges at her like a rabid dog, gnashing his teeth and clawing, both so savage, Father takes great strains tearing them apart.

Mother is shouting at them to stop, her face red and tear streaked. Gramma weeps, her soaking r's rolling in disbelief at her granddaughter's behavior. The other brothers yell at them, the baby howls, and Seamus shrieks at Rosa that he will kill her. Rosa looks up at her Father who is standing still between each of them held fast in his grip. She sees that he too is crying, and worse, has begun to shake. Slowly he releases his hold and without a sound drops to the floor, his body hiccuping.

This silences all, for never has he been seen to cry. It is too much to bear. Rosa fears her chest will crack open, spilling her guts out onto the linoleum.

She tears from the kitchen, through the dining room, the living room, the halls, and into her own room. She locks the door, pushes the bookcase in front of it, and the chest of drawers in front of that. She pulls off her clothes, crawls into bed, takes the pillow with her down under the blankets and weeps and weeps, saying the worst words she can imagine over and over with the pillow pressed hard against her mouth to muffle the sound. She is beyond redemption now and worse sin of all, she'd made Father cry. She weeps herself into a fitful sleep.

When she wakes it is dark and the house is quiet. She will not leave the room. First, because if Seamus sees her she'll be dead meat. Second, she is afraid to look into Father's eyes. Father is dying. Father is dying. She repeats this out loud to try and make sense of it. She cannot believe.

"Rosa, Rosa," calls Mother's voice from outside the barricaded door. "I'm going to bed now. Your dinner's on a plate in the oven."

Rosa holds her breath, unable to answer. Weary Mother turns away after another attempt and Rosa weeps again, regretting having hurt Seamus, and longing to be able to do the right thing. She can't help feeling that everything about her is wrong. And that is to be her punishment. Always doing the wrong thing. Making those around her miserable.

What is there in life to look forward to now? Why will God allow this to happen to Father? She presses her palms hard against the sides of her skull to push all thoughts away. Then she goes to the grate, lifts it, reaches down inside, and after a moment her fingers surface with a bottle of antacid. She hops onto her bed and sits cross-legged facing the window. The curtains are open. What she sees in the window pane is two fold. She sees the road, the entrance to the trail, the many familiar trees, and she sees her face, swollen and pale, the freckles standing out obliquely like Alder cones on the snow.

She unscrews the lid of the bottle, first using her teeth to break the seal. The liquid is thick and pink; she drinks the entire amount in one go. She replaces the lid, and as she leans closer to the window, resting her arms on the sill, it falls from the bed onto the floor. She doesn't notice. She lays her chin where her fingers weave to wait for the sickness in her belly that will soon come.

She thinks of the old oak tree. She feels its gnarled roots digging into her belly, tastes the rotting leaves stuffed into her mouth. Stupid. Little. Bitch. She whispers, each word punctuated by the crack of her chin on the sill. Crack. Crack. Crack. The last coming down with such a force her teeth crash together, sending shock waves through her spine.

༐

I WAS DROWNING. I had slipped, naked, into the black Humber, the winter Humber. For a time I floated, following peacefully with my mind as each part of me began to freeze. First my toes and fingertips, then my feet and hands. My nipples, my bum, my head, arms and legs. My vagina, frozen from the inside, felt like it would crack in two, the pain threatening to split my brain. The pain disappeared and I floated in the black water, the sky above dense like a gray wool blanket. And then the hole appeared, and my belly filled with water, water thick and itchy with old black bark and I began to sink down under the surface, down toward the tree graves. Before I hit the bottom, before the black became absolute, I saw something that terrified me. A tree, long ago murdered by a hand saw, rotted by water, forgotten by currents, had passed through my belly, clean through the hole. It passed through me, making its way toward

*the surface, my surface, while I sunk down, down
below the current, down into the grave.*

*Oh. There it is. I remember now. I remember what it
was that brought me to this room so early yesterday. If
smacking my head against this wall would make the truth
go away then I would smack and smack until my skull
cracked open and my bones smashed into ugly little
fragments. Smack until my brain spilled out and my
memory dispersed into tiny bubbles all over the floor, like
mercury from a thermometer. Nothing I can do, I fear, will
change what is. My Father is dying. My Father is dying.*

ক্সক্সক্স

"Rosa, move the furniture out of the way and let your
Father in."

Rosa opens her eyes to the dark, jumps up and begins
shoving the chest of drawers and the bookshelf back into
their proper places. She gets back into bed.

"Move over and give your Father a cuddle."

Such sweet words to hear. Here is Father, up to light
stoves before even the sun has woken, so that his
children's feet will press warm floors when the time
comes to rise. And what better forgiveness could there be
than this perfect place inside his arms?

"Rosa, I've got to go to Toronto in a few days to see
Granny. Would you like to come with me?" Of course,

she is thrilled by the prospect of taking her first steps on mainland soil.

"What about you?"

"I'll start the treatment when we get back."

Rosa flings herself at Father, hugging him tightly, breathing in the salty-sweet spruce tobacco smell of his skin. He pulls away, pats her head, and goes out to busy himself with morning. Rosa, now too excited to fall back to sleep, lays dreaming of what they'll see on this journey, and how different she'll be upon returning.

There have been travels before. Since she was nine, she, Seamus, and Jacob have spent six weeks every summer with their sister Elizabeth who lives on Nagles Hill in St. John's. The house had been built for a ship's captain more than a century before when fish were plentiful, and only a few had money. For three generations it has belonged to her brother-in-law Ron's family. Now the wind whips through holes in the plastic where the windows used to be. Rosa loves to wander through this house, hands outstretched, examining new shapes and textures. The smooth wooden balls at each end of the banister, the cold iron of the captain's bed, the painted talons at the base of the old pink bathtub. She fancies herself lady of this house in a time when it was grand, surveying the city from the top of the hill, waiting for love to sail home.

Ron is a mechanic and has a garage business next to the house overlooking a sea of car wrecks in the long yellow grassed field; acres of playground for visiting

children. There are many greased stained men and
brightly painted women who gather to smoke and drink
Pepsi. The men hang around the cars cursing and
laughing. Their wives gather in the kitchen; cigarettes
meeting crimson lips through loops of children's arms.

Rosa stands at the edge of these hours watching,
listening, remarking that her sister seems out of place in
this motley crew. Elizabeth has a bellow that rivals
Father's and when she laughs it is full and contagious, her
mouth cracking open, spilling a smile all over her face.

There is one woman in particular who fascinates.
Roxanne. Bob's skinny, overly made-up, raucous wife
who wears jeans so tight, they appear to have been
painted on, and drinks rum straight from a mickey. Her
many children vie for her attention, every summer a new
one. She comes, ebullient with the latest hilarious act of
one of these many; starting fires in her closet, baking the
cat, slicing off ear lobes, and other scandalous acts as she
follows Elizabeth around to whisper them in her ear.

Rosa spends her days walking the trails of Pippy Park
with her nieces and nephew in tow. She straps the baby
to her front, holds the girl by the hand, and follows the
boy through paths that lead to enchanted places.
Sometimes waterfalls, sometimes grassy fields, stunted
gnome-like woods, or the animal farm. At night there
will be treats of forbidden junk food, bars and chips, and
shows on cable she may watch even if there is kissing or
more. Such freedom.

She and her brothers camp in the upstairs landing, tucked into sleeping bags, telling fart and bum jokes. Rosa and Seamus take turns sending Jacob into fits of laughter. Soon they will begin longing for home, counting the days 'til the ten-hour bus trip back to Steady Brook, back to their parents' arms.

Rosa lies nestled in blankets, sheet folded over scratchy wool ones, meeting in perfect colour coordination the floral peach and green print bedspread Mother has made with matching curtains to celebrate the new room. Mother can work wonders on her old green Singer that came from Sears where Father works. She makes all of her own clothes, sometimes matching ones for Rosa. Rosa cherishes these moments; walking into Dominion to buy groceries, the two dressed in green straight legged pants and floral blouses with waist ties, holding hands and smiling at ladies who care to comment on how smart they look.

Mother is beautiful in her homemade clothes. No other woman compares. Rosa longs to crawl inside her, see out of her eyes, take comfort in her beliefs, and know what it is to be a woman. A woman who can do anything. Mother drives the car even though she's never had a license. Once they were stopped by the police who asked to see her papers. She got out of the car and started singing and dancing until the policeman became so embarrassed he drove away. Right on East Valley road in Corner Brook. Right in the open for anyone to see.

They go together to the Arts and Culture centre to hear music or to see plays. Rosa loves to look up at this glamour queen in her fur coat, high heels, and makeup to whom Father calls out from the wood pile:

"Tell me, my lady, how did an old wood cutter like me ever marry a woman as beautiful as you?"

Rosa hardly hears her reply as she watches in awe. She thinks it must be excellent to be rich and beautifully dressed in new garments at any hour of the day. As it is, apart from the ones Mother makes, her clothes are handed down from other families or ordered from the Sears catalogue and are never as good as she has imagined they will be.

From outside the door she hears the telltale sound of throat clearing and shuffling.

"Come on in and close the door, Jake."

His dimpled cheek appears around the corner.

"Oh. Hiya R-R-Rosa. You're awake already, are ya?"

"Yes, me buddy, now come in and sit down."

Jacob, smiling at the invitation, does as he is told and saunters over to the bed. He wears a navy dressing gown open over an undershirt tucked deep in his briefs, the elastic waist pulled as high as it will go. Rosa makes room and he sits. With his good hand, he reaches into the depths of his dressing gown, withdraws a piece of paper, and secreting it close to his chest, begins to giggle, the sound escaping his lips with a hiss.

"What's so funny, Jake?"

"Well, you see this here ticket I got right here?"

"Yup, I see it."

"Well, I got a good feeling about this here ticket. The draw's on S-S-Saturday night and you never know what might happen."

"What will you do with the money if you win, Jake buddy?"

"Well-l-l-l," he muses, the l lasting a season, "first I'd go straight to the bank and get it put on my bank book. Then aah probably go to the Jade Gardens for pork chops."

"What if you won a whole load of money, Jake? What would you spend it on?"

"Well, first I'd probably buy Mom and Dad a new car. Then maybe a new TV. But the draw's not till S-S-Saturday so I guess you'll have to wait 'til then to find out."

Jacob obsesses every week over the Saturday night draw, imagining his pockets heavy with riches, but he never wins more than two or ten dollars. The price of a ticket is the price of dreaming.

"S-s-so-o-o anyway, R-R-Rosa, yah, s-s-so-o-o ahhh, you got any good limericks for me to tell everybody at s-s-s-school?"

"Yeh, I do. I thought of one the other night but it's really dirty."

"Oh, is it?" his eyes twinkle, "how does it go?"

"Geeze, Jake I don't know if I should tell you, it's really bad."

"Ah, R-r-r-rosa, do I have to remind you that I'm a lot older than you? I'm 21-years-old you know s-s-so come on, let's have it."

"All right, Jake but you can't tell anyone that I made it up. Promise?"

Jacob promises and begins to giggle in anticipation of a good rhyme.

"There was an old woman named Nina." Jacob's body begins to shake at the mention of the name. "Who had such a stinky vagina." He loses it after she says that word and falls back against the wall, silently laughing, all teeth showing. "When she walked through the town, people fell to the ground, which amused that old woman named Nina."

Jacob laughs, hissing and spurting like a pot left to boil over on the stove. Finally composing himself, he asks Rosa to write it down so he can memorize it on the bus.

"Oh yah, R-r-r-rosa. The reason I came in here, hey, was to ahh tell you that you gotta get up for breakfast to practice for the Festival, the family songs, before s-s-s-school."

Right. The annual Rotary Music Festival, just the mention of which calls a nervous sweat to the surface of her skin, catching her in a quandary of revulsion and obligation. Every year she swears it will be her last to enter these torturous competitions, these exercises in public humiliation, yet, afraid of disappointing Mother and afraid of missing out on experiences deemed by adults to be valuable ones, she consents to be entered in numerous piano and singing classes and finds herself dreading the month of March with a passion.

This year the family will sing the Scottish 'Sky Boat' song and the Australian 'Waltzing Matilda'. Mother accompanies these melodies dressed to the nines. Last year she wore a royal blue, silver flowered blouse tucked snugly in a twenty-four inch waist electric blue camel fuzz skirt. They learn these songs painstakingly, all gathered in the living room around the piano, ears plugged to the others' harmony, with Andrew, the baby, only two, singing his own part.

Rosa adores this brother. His smiling eyes are large and such a deep brown they appear almost black. Since his birth he's possessed a full head of black hair. His skin is the darkest in the family, indeed he appears to have come from some hot and ancient land. Rosa loves to sit with him in her lap reading stories and breathing his scent. The scent is new life. Perfection. Promise.

In the kitchen all the family gather for breakfast. Seamus, like a dark cloud, glowers at Rosa from his seat by the stove. Rosa is relieved to see the damage to his scalp doesn't appear to be too serious.

"I'm sorry, Seamy. I'm really sorry."

Seamus shrugs and continues eating. Rosa despairs that that nothing she can do will make things right between them. And being the one to go with Father to Toronto will just fuel his resentment toward her.

On the way up to the bus stop she runs to catch up with him, determined to be friends again. Too much time has passed since they spent inseparable days together climbing trees and building snow forts, telling secrets and swearing loyalty. Somewhere along the way, perhaps too slowly to remark, she became a girl and he a teenager, and their only way of relating was to fight.

"Hey, Seamus, wait up!" she calls from the edge of the garden. He turns, surprised, and waits for her to reach him.

"You asshole, I got holes in my head because of you!" He shoves her, not hard, on the shoulder, and turns back to the road.

"Seamus, I did it because you made me so mad. And I did it because I was mad about everything. It's not my fault you lost your room, I'm a girl, damn it! I can't go sharing a room with the boys all my life. That would be gross."

"You got to learn to control your temper."

"Yeah? So do you."

They walk in silence for a time, their breath pushing out clouds in the early morning air, pausing in synch to look out over the river, resplendent in an ice trimmed coat.

"Seamus, what do you think is going to happen to him?"

"Ahh, he'll be all right. If he stops smoking."

"Yeah. He'll be all right." She says this not because she believes it, but in order to believe.

"But he'll never stop smoking."

They turn to see the bus pulling into the stop and are off running as fast as the snow covered road will allow without pitching them skyward, Rosa's heart soaring when Seamus grabs the fur rimmed cuff of her coat, pulling her to keep up with him.

ৡৡৡ

I dreamt tonight that he was dead. He was dead and came back to see us. He made a camp for the dead out in the garden, over near the wood pile. He lived inside and would call out to us all night long. Calling out our names within his death camp until sleep was impossible. We all gathered in the kitchen, the only light from the fire in the woodstove, and stood in silence listening to his calling. At each name we looked at the one who was called, saying nothing. And when they stayed within we were relieved. Each of us secretly relieved. And the calling went on and on and it was torture to hear yet we could not shut our ears against it. What really disturbs me about this dream is that when his calling stopped I felt happy. I felt happy that I could go back to my bed and sleep for hours more. I was going to sleep long and deep and think no more of him out there in the cold, alone in the realm of the dead, refused by his family.

And now that I am awake I am crying for the guilt of this dream. If I could dream it again I would go to him. I would bring hot tea and warm brown bread. I would bring wool socks and a soft blanket and go out into the garden in my bare feet and when I knocked on the door of his camp he would open it and lift me up as easily as if I were a little child again. We would laugh like old friends and I would ask him to tell me one more time about the Albino moose and I would pretend to believe. I would ask him why he burned the ski-do and he would tell me the truth. We would walk along the red sandy beach of the river, just at the pebbly edge of the water, telling stories and laughing until the early hours of the morning. Then seeing him in the moments before full dawn, I would see that death had only changed him a little, in an almost unrecognizable way. And only then would I sleep, long and deep.

ॐ

ON THE APPOINTED DAY, Rosa carefully folds
selected outfits into a plaid canvas duffel bag along
with a book of myths, four Nancy Drews, and the
black book of secrets. These are placed in the car
along with Father's things, blankets, pillows, and
food. The journey will take three days. Her
excitement is at such a pitch she fears she will cry.
After clutched goodbye's and waves back to
everyone standing at the road until the car is out of
sight, she faces forward to welcome in adventure.

The sun over the hills through western Newfoundland augurs a good passage over the Gulf. Father tells her
about how the mountain ranges on this side of the island
are a part of the Appalachians that extend from Europe
to Alabama. Ours are low and flat on top, razed by ice
age glaciers, cleft with fjords, rich with life. For much of
the three-hour drive, unpopulated land extends for as far

as the eye can see. In the distance, the hills are patchy, scarred by clear-cutting, trees plucked out by mechanical harvesters like unwanted hairs.

As the sun sets they reach Port-Aux-Basques, a seaport town of happily painted wooden structures standing precariously on the rocks at the edge of a forbidding sea. The ferry, the "Joseph and Clara Smallwood" is one of the largest boats she has seen, even bigger than the Russian paper ships that dock in Corner Brook harbour.

They drive the car on to the boat and leave it parked in the bowels of the ship. After a time they find their way to a cabin with a porthole, bunk beds, and bars of soap wrapped in stiff blue paper. Rosa lies on her belly in the top bunk, thrilled by the waves crashing against the window, and the languorous lurching of the ship that will carry them to the fabled mainland. She reaches her hand down for Father to hold. He closes his book, envelopes her hand completely in his, and begins to tell her a story.

"There once was a girl named Maria who lived in a little cabin with her Mother, Father, two sisters and a brother on the shores of the Great Northern Peninsula. They lived all alone in the town which is now called Cow Head. It was so named by her father for the night he was caught in a terrible storm coming home from pulling in his lobster pots. The sky suddenly went dark, as if it were an eyeball over which a lid had shut. The waves tossed his boat about so fiercely, the lobster were sprung from their pots, and he was thrown overboard. He tried to swim, but the sea was too angry, forcing itself down into his lungs. He was sure he'd die when, at the last possible moment, a massive cow appeared in the air above him. She was as long as two dories, her girth as great as an oil tanker, with knotted woolly hair in which eagles had built their nests, and her horns like two giants had perched themselves on either side of her head. The wondrous cow picked the man up with her horns, carried him over the raging waters, and left him belching brine but very much alive on the shore of Shallow Bay.

In the morning he was awakened by his wife who, along with the children, had been out looking for him all night. He told her what had happened and they named that part of the coast in the magical cow's honour, for they believed she lived on the wild part of the land that juts out into the sea."

"What about Maria?"

"Hold on now, I'm getting to that."

"Maria was the oldest of the children and worked hard everyday; mending nets, salting fish, sometimes working on the boat alongside her father. She would cry when the salt stung her hands that were split from toil. She dreamed of leaving the little cove, wearing fine dresses, and seeing the world. This desire was so fierce in her she would promise herself every night she would leave, spitting and rubbing her palms together to make the promise stick.

One day a ship sailed into the bay. When it left three days later, Maria was on it with scarcely a goodbye to her family. She travelled far and wide, to lands great and small, fantastical and horrible. Yet, wherever she went, the same phenomenon occurred. The first three days in a new place were always happy ones. So many new sights, people, languages, and food. However, on the fourth day, an intense sadness overwhelmed her, a terrible yearning for something she could not identify. She stayed until her unhappiness was so extreme that she felt she surely would perish were she to remain another day. So she moved on to a new city, and country, yet, wherever she went, the panic followed her, undermining her happiness. Never could she discover the cause of her anguish.

Years passed. One day while she sat by the sea, staring out the window of another room in another town, a storm blew in. Waves beat on the shore, making great cracking sounds as they smacked off the rocks. As the sky went dark, Maria remembered a night long ago when she combed the shores of Newfoundland looking for her father. She remembered the cove, the little house, her mother, brother, and sisters. She began to weep, and weep, perhaps for joy of finally understanding where her longing came from, and why she was so drawn to the sea. Her tears poured forth in such abundance that they swelled beneath her, carrying her into the sea, and back to the little cottage in Cow Head. Her family was overjoyed to see her, and there Maria stayed. For gone was the yearning, gone was her anguish, and here were the things she had been desiring all along: the company of loved ones, the land of her birth that moved her more profoundly than even the most splendid places she had seen, and the North Atlantic ocean."

Father stands up and tucks Rosa in, then gets back into his own bunk. Both are lulled to sleep, rocked in the arms of the sea.

In the morning, after leaving the boat, they drive through North Sydney, Nova Scotia, and into New Brunswick. There is something different about this mainland. Something in the sameness of the land, in the neatness and uniformity of the houses, in the shiny new cars that sparkle along highways that, for the most part, are amazingly free of bumps and potholes.

After a full day of driving, they stop at a motel for the night. A room with two double beds covered in orange nubbly spreads, a bathroom and television. Each lies in their own bed and watch a doctor named Quincy solving crimes and performing autopsies. After the show, Father pats her back, kisses her goodnight on the top of her head, and turns out the light. Rosa lies awake in the vast bed trying to identify the feeling in her belly. There are words just behind the surface of her lips that want to take form and sound, but cannot find impetus. Words that might explain her anxiety, so that he would know what had happened to her. And somewhere amongst all these unspoken words scattered like fragments of a puzzle are questions to do with why this thing had to happen to her and why he wasn't there to save her from what no child should have to experience. She feels a mixture of love and fear and anger toward him. Yet the worst of these feelings is the not knowing what will happen to him, what will happen to them all.

Father coughs. Deep, rumbling, racking coughs. Phlegmy barking. Rattling his body that twists and spasms until finally he spews in the sink what is only a symptom of the deeper problem. Rosa, eyes wide open in the dark room, bites her fingers to keep from crying out. Father gets back into bed and, after a time, succumbs to sleep. She thinks it odd that there are two beds, and sleeps only after Father begins to snore.

In the car he asks:

"What is it you write about in that black book of yours?"

"Ummm," she stalls, unsure of how to talk about what has always been her secret. "My dreams mostly, I guess. When I wake in the middle of the night, I write down what I've been dreaming or thinking about."

"What do you dream about?"

"Do you mean at night, or during the day?"

"Both. Tell me what's on your mind, my dear one."

"Well," she says, feeling her face grow hot, "at night I have these weird dreams. They wake me up and the only way for me to sleep again is to write them down. It's like they are really happening to me."

"What sort of things happen in your dreams?"

"Well, for example, a little while ago I saw you watching the ski-doo burn at the back of the garden. In my dream, I was lost and tried to sleep at the edge of a pond. I couldn't sleep because of the fire and I saw you, really just the shadow of you, watching it burn. And not doing anything."

"Did that bother you?"

"Well, I guess so, because I don't know why you did that."

"Maybe I don't know why either."

She doesn't believe him. She understands something about the need for lies to the self to comfort the conscience and says no more about it. She watches him light a cigarette, the action so familiar, he doesn't need to take his eyes off the road.

"Father, are you going to quit smoking?"

He doesn't answer. He watches the road, his stillness only broken by the left hand movement to his mouth, up and away, up and away, flick out the window, up and away.

They arrive in Toronto the next night. Father's sister Sara welcomes them into the apartment she shares with Granny. Sara is a nun but dresses like a normal person and doesn't pepper her conversation with references to God. She looks and laughs a lot like Father, and when she smiles there is a very un-nun like gleam in her eye. Rosa wonders why she joined the convent in the first place since nuns had to practice celibacy and go to mass every day of the week, not just on Sundays. She knows girls aren't supposed to ask such questions. Not where God and Jesus and the blessed Virgin Mary are concerned. No doubts. No queries. Obey. Believe.

Ancient Granny of ninety-five lies on the couch where she stays most of the time. Tea bags on eyes to soothe, she speaks animatedly with her friend Napoleon Bonaparte, and tries in vain to remember the names of her family; Rosa wonders why Granny can only remember the names of the dead. Rosa recalls hearing of a time when Granny lived in Corner Brook in a house that overlooked the cemetery by the Knights of Columbus building. She awoke in the middle of the night and went out into the snow wearing only a nightie to rescue a statue of the Virgin Mary. Bring the poor girl in from the cold.

During the afternoons, Rosa walks the streets holding her Father's hand, all senses full of the market. There are so many people. So many lovely colours of skin; black as the raised keys on the piano, skin that makes her long to reach out her hands to warm herself in its exotic heat. There are other colours; hues of amber she imagines would taste of sweetest candy. These women, Father whispers, are Oriental. Oriental, Rosa repeats to herself, feeling the shape of this word. A new place for the list of *Someday*.

"Would you like to try a pomegranate?" he invites. Her mouth opens like a teacup into which he pours red bejeweled seeds that burst and spill sweetly over her tongue, the inside bits sticking between her teeth. She feels such profound happiness, as if her bones are singing songs to her. Everywhere she looks is something new. Something called avocados, mushrooms that don't come in cans, florets of broccoli, fresh, not frozen, royal purple bulbs called eggplants, and rounds of white cheese the size of car tires. Here begins a new list of *Beautiful Fruits and Vegetables* and *Other Fine Things to Eat*.

"We've been away for over a week. Are you homesick yet?" Father wonders.

"No. I don't miss it one little bit."

"Well, you will. I've never met a Newfoundlander that was happy living anywhere else. You aren't aware of it yet. What home means. What that island means to you. You dream of getting out, I can see that. Go. Do it when the time comes. But you won't be happy living anywhere else for long, I can guarantee you that. It's in your blood. In a secret place in that brooding heart of yours it lives. It's there and you won't ever get rid of it. Home."

Rosa stares up at him silently. The skin around his eyes is yellow. She takes his hand and presses it to her cheek.

ৡৡৡ

I am awake here in my bed on the floor. Around the corner Granny murmurs in her sleep, words I can only half understand. I don't think she can really be sleeping while she talks so much. I hope she doesn't notice me. She doesn't know who I am. And I'm a little frightened of her. When I woke up I was crying. I dreamt that we returned to the valley only to find an army of mechanical harvesters had come, side-by-side, numbering in the hundreds, from over the mountains across the river, ripping out every tree as they came. The sound was murderous. We covered our ears and ran through the trail to the riverbank and when we saw what was coming we must have started screaming, but could hear nothing over the mechanical grind that clear cut through the valley. Every tree on the other side had been cut and stacked neatly in piles on the ground. Then the machines began to cross over the river. We stood watching with horror as they advanced toward us. We could not move. They came then, all in a line up over the bank, ripping up trees, their roots snapping, bloodlines severed, histories lost. Still, we stood together unable to move. They ripped us up, too, and we were thrust aside, crushed, severed, our last thoughts of the garden and how it would be destroyed, all our beautiful trees, lifelong friends, and how the harvesters would continue on over Marble mountain and on and on murdering a doomed foreverness of forest, their greed never satisfied. I would rather be dead than live to see that ugliness in our valley, like the razed hills of the upper Humber, destroyed by the greed of the machines. I cried for a long time trying to overcome this panic, this fear that everything will be gone when we get back. I want to go home. I want to see my valley and the river, Mother and Gramma, and the boys. I miss the mountains, and long to be within their circle.

ন্থ্ৰ্থ্ৰ

It is time to go, for Father's treatment must begin. He says goodbye in a serious way, holding his mother and then his sister a long time in his arms. Sara makes the sign of the cross on his head as Rosa and Father leave.

Driving back into Steady Brook after a ten-day absence, she behaves as one who has been away for a very long time, greeting lovingly all of the cherished childhood places. There is the trail that leads to the Tarzan tree. A lone paper birch precarious on the lip of ravine over which she and the boys fly, clutching fast to a thick rope, sometimes two at a time. What a thrill it is even when someone knocks the wind out of themselves. There is the mouth of Steady Brook where the floods used to come every spring. Where they build rafts and float out to the river, jumping off into shoulder high water before reaching the current. Here is home, nestled safely in the Humber Valley, between the brook and the river. This is the place that will soon become all too familiar again, and her yearning for unknown lands will begin anew.

Father's treatment begins, and his body bears obvious evidence of disease. His hair falls out, even his eyebrows and lashes. His face assumes a pallid mask. Moving so deliberately, often in hospital for short stays, this new reality of Father cannot be reconciled with the old familiar one. Little pieces of him are leaving every day. Where is he going?

Under the cold comfort of their snow forts, Rosa and the younger brothers like to tell stories of the old Father. Stories that begin, remember the time? and end with forced laughter. Laughter practiced to give the illusion of normalcy. Laughter practiced to build security. Laughter to convince their secret hearts that the world isn't dying quickly around them.

Remember the time he wore a leotard, pink tutu, and slippers to the Boxing Day dinner with the nuns from All Hallows Convent? When all were seated in the dining room neatly around the twelve-foot table, he appeared in full ballet regalia, beer in hand, cigarette in mouth, offering his own special interpretation of Swan Lake. And weren't the Sisters rendered speechless? And wasn't *that* a good time?

These stories revive for only fleeting moments the memory of the Father that was. For this Father is changing beyond recognition. This Father, whose knees hurt when sat upon, who rarely laughs, who is impatient, who can't cut wood, whose body is disintegrating a little every day, who is beginning to resemble pictures she has seen at school of concentration camp victims from the Second World War. Unspeakable horrors. Unspeakable fears.

Still, there is school in the mornings, supper in the evenings, and lessons continue as usual. Mother spends more and more time away from home tending to Father in the hospital and taking night classes at the university. Rosa takes advantage of these times to slip into their bedroom, run her fingers over the curled mahogany furniture, a suite it is called, and look in dark drawers at secret things. A choker, mother of pearl shells hung on a silk rope, rings of jewels, tins of pictures, black and white, of ladies with hats and sturdy shoes, men in shirts and ties, holding babies and smoking. She stands in the closet amid dresses and shoes, trying favourites on, wondering when they'll fit.

The chest at the foot of the bed, gray ribbed with wood, when opened emanates forth sweet aged scents: treasured fabrics, furs, babies christening dresses, candles, and wool. Rosa sits and breathes deeply of this perfume. The scent is of years of family, years of hope. The loveliest object is the lady sculpture that sits on a dish in which Mother keeps everyday jewelry. Her long hair drapes over her shoulder to cover her breasts, her round belly catches a diaphanous skirt beneath which her shapely legs extend to reveal bared elegant feet. Rosa runs her fingers over the perfect contours of this miniature clay woman until she hears the car pulling into the driveway. She slips out quickly before the door opens to Mother, tired and sad, smiling with her mouth but not her eyes. And throughout the house there is the tension of waiting. Waiting for things to get worse as Gramma warns of how little money there will be when . . . The words left unspoken.

This tension manifests itself in Rosa as a desire to alter her state of being. Lack of sleep succeeds in this as does eating two handfuls of chewable vitamin C. The latter makes her so wretchedly ill that her own well-being is all she can focus on. The former is an older, darker, more pernicious drug and cannot be controlled like the simple eating of noxious substances. Her nocturnal writings are barely legible. Her anxiety increases.

What is happening to us? What is happening to Father? I am afraid to sleep these days and so pass the nights fully dressed sitting up in my bed, the curtains drawn, dozing in and out of sleep, waiting for something to happen. I got so worried last night that I ate two handfuls of vitamin C. The chewable kind. And I got so damn sick I thought I might die. I don't think anyone even noticed. That's O.K. because the last thing I want is to have to talk about what's going on. And there is that other thing that won't go away. I wish I could fill up that hole and be finished with it. I wish this last year could disappear and things could be like they were when Father was himself and there wasn't this uncertainty. That's a fantasy and I don't know what we'll do if things keep on this way. Mother says we must trust in God. I wish I could.

Rosa closes her book, puts it back under the grate and opens the door, listening in the dark. Nothing stirring. She takes her winter coat and pants down from the nail upon which they hang and slips back into her room. Thinking her boots are out in the back porch and too much of a risk to retrieve, she puts on thick wool socks and running shoes and opens the window. It is a short jump to the hardened crust of snow. Rosa wades hip-deep through it, past the pine trees, ducking under their heavily laden branches, and out to the road. It is sweet to be out in the night air. The sky is black, infinite, the stars sticking out like luminous silver freckles.

She makes her way, crunching over the hard packed snow to Falls Avenue, continues on to the brook and sits on the cement wall, built a decade ago to hem the waters in. Pitching backward into the snow, she makes an angel, then lies still, arms and legs extended, staring into the sky, losing herself in it.

It is the cold flakes on her face that wake her and she sits up with a start, frightened and disoriented. It is still dark, near the end of winter, but still bloody cold. Rosa runs toward the house, running to create some warmth, and when she reaches the back end of the garden, she climbs over the snowbank, cutting through the trees. Moving laboriously through the garden, on toward the kitchen lamplight that spills out onto the snow, her stomach tightens for a moment. Seeing that light, she wonders if something has happened, if an alarm has been raised. But all is quiet. She moves closer to the window. Mother is sitting in her armchair with a straight-backed chair pulled in front of her. A skein of wool is stretched over the back. Rosa finds the repetitive movements of her Mother almost hypnotic as she pulls off a round of wool, once twice, then pauses to roll it in the ball. The wool is Briggs Little two-ply pure wool from New Brunswick. Mother never knits with synthetic yarns. She says Briggs Little is the best value for the money. And it must be green. Stretch forward, wind once, twice, sit back and wind around and around the ball. Rosa stands transfixed, watching her Mother's efficient, graceful movements, her so lovely on display in the lamplight.

Mother looks up. She sits frozen for a moment, then stands and moves slowly to the window, reaching to extinguish the light without taking her eyes off of Rosa. She takes her daughter's hand in hers and leads her to the woodstove, only breaking contact long enough to move the armchair close to the fire. She sits and pulls Rosa onto her lap. Through the glass they watch the fire. The flames cast long flickering shapes on the walls. A moody shadow play. Mother speaks:

"You're still a little girl, yet your worries make you look old beyond your years."

"I'm ugly," Rosa moans and begins to cry, burying her face in her Mother's chest.

"Shh. You are beautiful, my little one, my pretty pink rosebud. You are my special beauty. Don't say things like that about yourself. Where were you?"

"I couldn't sleep so I went down to the brook and I just dozed off for a minute."

"You mustn't go out by yourself at night, Rosa. It's not right. Why can't you sleep?"

"I'm worried," she whispers, and begins to cry again.

"I suppose we all are. But whatever happens we must trust in God. You must give all your worries to him, he will take them away to the farthest reaches of the earth where they will have no power over you. He will comfort you. He will bring you peace."

Rosa has no reply to this. They sit, staring into the fire, rocking slightly back and forth, back and forth. After a while, Mother speaks.

"There's so little time these days for this. For just sitting together. Talking and sitting. There is so little time."

"What are you knitting now?"

"A sweater for your Father. He's always wanted an Irish knit pullover to wear in the woods."

"What's the pattern?"

"It's called a fisherman knit. It's made up of a series of knots and chains that resemble the knots the Irish fishermen used. It's a very old design. It's like a code."

"It sounds like magic."

"I hope it is," she sighs. The moment is broken by the sound of Father's coughing, weak and ineffectual. Rosa finds herself coughing for him, wishing he could get up what wants to come up. Rosa watches her Mother's expression as she looks past her into the fire. It appears serene. Her hands, however, are seized and tense, like the talons of a bird of prey, one of them gripping the fleshy part of Rosa's arm so that she must will herself to keep silent. To Rosa these hands betray an unspeakable angst. Her Mother's hands are artist's hands, not only in what they are capable of creating, but in how they interpret the secrets of her heart. These hands, she understands for the first time, watching them with wonder, are a window to the very essence of Mother.

ও

"ROSA. ROSA. DID YOU TAKE MY CIGARETTES?
Where did you put my cigarettes?"

Without a word, Rosa gets up, takes her Father's
hand, leads him through the halls, through the living and
dining rooms, through the kitchen, into the old
bathroom, reaches behind the toilet, and pulls out a near
full pack of Export A, dark green. She hands them over,
her bottom lip quivering, the threat of tears stinging her
nose.

Father and daughter stand in the emerging dawn
meeting eyes. Rosa's seek acknowledgment of this
betrayal, Father's respond that there is no use, no help,
death is coming.

In the kitchen, Father pours the tea into cups. The
steam from the tea rises to engage in a macabre dance
with the smoke from his cigarette, until he takes a drag,

the new smoke forcing the dancers off the floor. Rosa thinks he looks like a wizened dragon.

"Rosa, when I'm gone."

"Oh Father, don't."

"Just listen to me now. Lend your old man an ear, will you? This isn't going to go away. I don't think I'll live to see the summer. I need you to look after things for me. Look after the boys. Help your Mother as much as you can. And remember these words, Rosa: If you want to fly with the eagles, don't hang out with the turkeys. Rosa?"

"Yes, Father, I will." she promises through lips wet with tears. She wipes them away with the back of her hand, her sleeve catching the running of her nose.

"Come here, my girl, and give us a cuddle."

"Doesn't it hurt?" Rosa inquires of sitting on his lap.

"Naaa." he protests, and she understands that he is lying.

"Father, where do think you'll . . . go?" she asks, afraid to say the word.

"I think I'll be like the wind, able to move at will. I'll fly over the mountains to Grand Lake. I'll move through trees, rest on the backs of caribou, and hover over the Atlantic watching storms blow up, being tossed about and laughing my love, and laughing."

"Do you believe in heaven?"

"Well, I think that will be heaven. I'll be free."

Rosa steps down from her Father's lap, for she feels him wincing in pain. She places her hand on his knee to lean over to kiss him, then quickly withdraws it, for all she feels is the bone under a thin layer of skin. Gone is the flesh. She regards him unflinchingly, and in that moment, he appears as ancient as the hills.

The next few days bring the feared piano competitions in the Rotary Music Festival. First comes the hated *Fantasia*. Rosa perches on a black stool, hands sweaty and shaking, playing slippery notes on the grand piano on stage at the Arts and Culture centre. She is dressed in a red wool sweater and a kilt with matching cape that Gramma had brought from Scotland more than forty years before. It had first been worn by Gramma, then Mother, then four sisters, and now by Rosa who wishes, each time her memory of music falters, that the black stage boards would open to swallow her up and deliver her unembarrassed to Father who, sitting at the back of the theater for as long as he could without being sick, would take her home.

The next class would bring much needed and long awaited success. Bartok's *The Bears* is the set piece. Percussive banging of left hand chords, violent and powerful she dances grizzlies and blacks over the back hills of Marble Mountain, leaving them to fish in the secret lake that will yield plenty. First place, only this once making the torture worthwhile. Afterward she sits proud in the front seat between her parents, celebrating with mint green St. Paddy's Day milkshakes from the drive through at McDonald's. This is to be Father's last outing, for the cancer has caught him in its malignant trap.

He is relegated to a hospital bed placed at the foot of one shared for more than thirty years of marriage and baby making behind the closed door of his room around which silence is asked and given. Rosa slips into this place of abnormal quiescence, clinical smells, and sits beside her Father. She presses her head to his, passing on the warmth of her youth. She caresses his scalp that is now adorned with fuzz like a baby's, singing a dirty song in his ear:

Me and you and a dog named Blue,
jumped around and did our Poo.

She dares to hope he will bellow like a savage and call for Dr. Murphy. The old joke he used to play when little ones were unruly. Cupping hand to mouth, he'd make megaphone echoes, calling one who would administer imaginary punishment, and they would behave. No bellow now solicits proper behavior.

Young ones unsure of how to act gather to visit Father during his short stays for treatment in the hospital in a room shared with a withered man who smokes cigarettes through a tube stuck in a hole cut out of his throat. When he comes home again, visiting is shared between older ones, newly arrived, and younger ones, displaced in their roles, languishing for the old play of life.

Mary has come. The adored sister with lush golden hair that stretches down, gathering in unison where her broad back curves into a slender waist. Rosa recalls watching from Manuel's beach how Mary, while filling buckets when the capelin ran, had been whistled at by fishermen passing in their boats. How could they resist paying homage to this goddess in a blue and white bikini; strength of man married with grace of woman? Mary will entertain the boys with songs and feats of "G.I. Jen", transcending the machismo and violence of dolls boys cherish, reducing them to giggles of admiration and awe.

Greta comes. Smart, lovely, and freckled as ever. She will sleep in Rosa's bed, displacing her to a blanketed lawn chair beside it. Rosa doesn't mind as Greta sends her lovely gifts of soapstone boxes and silk scarves. She tells her stories of Mirabel the princess and cooks exotic foods. There comes Elizabeth who is warm and efficient, who organizes a clean sweep of the house, even getting the boys involved. Catherine arrives, and with her magical voice sits at the piano to sing to this house where music has ceased to live.

The sisters tell stories of hard lives. They tell of different standards for boys and girls. They tell how meat sandwiches were given to boys to bring for school lunches while girls had to make do with jam and peanut butter. Girls had to clean the house from top to bottom while boys carried on as they pleased. They won't forget. Ways will be changed for their children. You've got it easy, they say. Times were harder for us.

Privacy is impossible to find in the house now as there is only so much space in which to contain all the various personalities of Mother and Father's prolific union. Rosa's need to write and wander is curtailed. She wakes to cluttered household sounds. Teaspoons clicking cups, fry pans frying, and sisters debating strategies of cleaning up this mess of a home. Boys demand food and are fed first, as is always the way, then quickly clear out to evade enlistment in "women's work". Rosa stands at the sink, slowly making a dent in the piles of egged, greased up, tea stained dishes, listening to the sisters criticisms of the low hygienic standards of the young ones. Rosa feels all the heat in her body rise into her head. She whips around to face the critics, her green eyes flashing like the lights on a marquee. In words she wishes were brilliant and damning, but are more the impassioned stops and starts of a little girl, she silences them.

"You don't even live here. It's none of your business how dirty we are. You . . . We . . . This is our home and none of you understand anything. You're all . . . Look . . . WHY DON'T YOU JUST GET LOST YOU BUNCH OF JERKS!" she screams in a raw voice, and tears from the room.

In a few days, reconciled older ones leave, allowing the young ones to stretch out and reclaim their cluttered corners. Father's sickness is worsening a little each day, as if his life is a sea that only ebbs, never flows, receding into an ignominious puddle. His skin that was once tough like leather, always deep red in the places he kept exposed to the sun, is now thin and dry, like withered leaves blown about the garden after their autumnal splendor has faded. There are places on his body where the skin has ceased to join. These chasms grow wider each day. It is hard to look at him now, hard to watch the anger and shame that flare briefly in his sunken eyes. Throughout the house they wait.

The older brothers come to see Father. Paul, the eldest, who has muscles the young ones like him to flex. Then Matthew, who hasn't been seen in a long time. Then Mark, whom Rosa can hardly remember. He is tall, dark, and lean and looks like Father. He works as a logger deep in the forests of British Columbia. They gather to hear Mark tell of the time he was chased by a grizzly as large as a house. When he makes the sound of the bear breathing down his neck they scream until he stops, then ask him to tell it again. Soon these ones leave too, and the waiting resumes.

ৰৰৰ

One afternoon early in the spring, Rosa, Seamus, Angus, and Jacob find themselves walking together from the bus stop toward the house. They walk in silence, spanning the width of the road, stopping in unison when they reach the river. They stand, backs to the road and the boisterous carryings on of the other children who make their way home through the snow, bodies to the river, faces upturned toward the mountains beyond. It must be ages they stand like this, for when Jacob speaks, there are no other children to be heard.

"The ice is all broke up now. I bet Father'll be glad to get the boat out this S-S-Spring." They all turn to look at Jacob.

"For God's sake, Jake, he's too damn sick to take a walk anymore, let alone go out in the boat," says Seamus, shaking his head in disbelief.

"Oh yeah," says Jacob, "I s-s-s-suppose you're right about that."

"You shouldn't talk like that about him," flares Angus. "You shouldn't make it seem like there's no hope. He might get better. Dr. McLaren even said so."

"That was way back in the beginning when he was first diagnosed! Don't you get it?" Seamus' voice is high and unnatural. "HE'S NOT GOING TO GET BETTER!" he shouts at Angus.

"SHUT UP SEAMUS, YOU SHITTHEAD!" yells Rosa.

"Yeah, Seamus, you jerk, how can you say that about him?" says Angus, beginning to cry.

"Because it's true, you bunch of babies! Why do you think he's stopped going to the hospital for treatment?" Seamus is crying now. "HE'S DYING! HE'S DYING!" He shrieks. Angus charges at him, plowing into his gut and knocking them both to the ground. They punch at one another, both in tears. Rosa jumps in, trying to pry them apart, and yelling at them to stop. Then she starts hitting, too, not knowing where her punches land, and crying right along with them. A raw howl, the sound seeming as wide as the river, tears over them, stopping them dead. Involuntarily they all raise their hands to their ears to shut out the sound, like screaming blood. They turn toward Jacob, his hands aloft in the air, his right arm, the little one, stuck out at a right angle to his body, the hand swinging up and down along with his voice. Long after the fighting has ended, he stops howling and begins to walk unsteadily away, then turns back to look at them.

"Stop fightin' you bunch of meatheads! You crowd of liver lips! Just sssstop fightin' all right? Come on," he says to them, giving an order. "You get crazy like that again and I'll kill you all. Now get moving." They get up and move, just like Jacob told them to and when they reach the house, no one mentions the fight, and no one mentions Father's health again.

ॐॐॐ

I dreamt tonight that we were buried alive. All of us, deep in the ground, our mouths stuffed with rotted leaves, clawing at the earth for a bit of space to breath. Somehow we were all able to see one another and the fear in our eyes burned into my brain so that I could never forget what it was to watch us all die and to feel it myself. I know what this means. I know what is happening in this house. Everything hopeful and happy and youthful about us is seeping away along with Father's health. Everyday as a little more of him dies, so a little more of us dies. Only you can't see it. It's happening inside. Inside where it can't be named or treated. Inside where it can't be seen with an x-ray. Inside in a secret place that's not polite to talk about. The stench of death is about us, it permeates this house, it has seeped into our insides. It has infected us all. People sense it. It makes them uncomfortable. Not in a way they can articulate. Not in a way we can articulate to one another. We are all alone together with our dying. We are heavy with it. So heavy that to lie upon a bed to sleep is an exhausting endeavor. I haven't the energy. I will never sleep again. I will never be happy again. I haven't the taste for it. All I taste is death.

When I sit here like this, facing the window, the curtains drawn, I can see into the trail. As far as the first bend in the path I see. After that I can close my eyes and imagine it all. I know every tree in there. If I allow myself I can really feel what it is to walk through the trail, can make real the branches brushing my face, can hear the leaves crunch beneath my feet. The trail was a good place full of pleasant associations. Quiet times by myself, or playful ones with the boys. But the other thing, the thing I will not remember, has ruined it all for me. Now it is a place of murky, nightmarish fear. A place of guilt. A place of sickness. And I know when it changed. That's when this all began. That's when I stopped sleeping. I want to go back to how it was before. I want to go back to feeling the simple things a child feels without all this extra weight that pulls me down, underneath the living, and makes me feel so heavy, like being under water.

ख़

IN THE MORNING, BEFORE THE ACCUSTOMED
HOUR, Gramma comes to usher the young ones out
of bed and into Mother and Father's room. They
gather by the cold steel hospital bed in the new
spring light of dawn, rubbing sleep from their eyes,
and nudging with elbows and shoulders for a place
next to Father's bed.

"Look!" whispers Mother, gesturing with wonder to
the garden beyond the window. There before them is
what until now has existed only in the never-never
baloney bog world of Father's fancy. They stand silent,
awe-struck, watching steam cloud-puffing through the
nostrils of this magnificently antlered Albino moose,
bucking in the patchy spring snow. He passes close to the
window, crazy-eights through the garden, then throws
his great white head back in a bellow they can hear even
through the steamed up window. He turns his regal head

toward them, stares for a moment with his red-rimmed brown eyes like massive pools of coffee into which one could dive and never reach the bottom, then gallops on endless legs out of the garden and on towards the mountains. The delighted audience breaks into vocal applause for this treat and are hushed-hushed out of the room. Rosa lingers a moment, kisses Father's chalky cheek, and leans in close to whisper in his ear.

"I will always believe you."

She feels the sudden and intense need to protect him. He is so small lying there, so shrunken and fragile, almost repulsive in this wretched state. But there is nothing she can think of to do. She leaves the room, goes into the kitchen, pours herself a sugary cup of tea, and sits in the chair that is called Father's, watching snow fill in the tracks of their morning visitor.

After a time, the bedroom door opens and Mother emerges wrapped in her shiny blue dressing gown. Her face divided by ribbons of tears, she presses her wet cheeks to Rosa's.

"Oh my darling," she whispers, holding Rosa to her breast, the only sound is of breath. Rosa feels a growing emptiness in her belly, as if a tractor is plowing her guts out of the way to make room for pain.

"He's gone?" she asks, already knowing the answer. Mother nods.

"I'll go tell the boys," she offers as comfort, leaving Mother to deal with the adult business of making calls to people who will come to take Father's body away.

She moves slowly through the house, possessed by a dull calm. The waiting is over. The unspoken has proclaimed itself as real as the weather and she feels no response but an unnatural calm. She enters the boys' rooms, first Seamus and Jacob's, then Angus and Andrew's, and tells them that Father is dead. There are no tears or tantrums. Words that want to be grown up express old fashioned sentiments like, "he's better off" and "at least he's not suffering." They all file into the kitchen where Mother kneels to light the woodstove, and take turns cuddling with her and Gramma. Soon the silent ambulance arrives. Father's shrunken body is carried out on a stretcher and driven away.

Rosa goes into the hall where many old clothes hang on hooks, and takes down warm things to wear outside. She slips out of the house, down Falls Avenue to the brook, and over newly exposed rocks to the mouth where she drops, splitting the thin ice with her knees, and weeps. When her tears are exhausted she lies with one cheek pressed to a rock and falls asleep.

When she wakes, the morning has already slipped into afternoon, and the gray threat of early evening oppresses the sky. This is her first thought, resentment toward the day that passes too soon into night. Now comes the remembrance of what had brought her out, and the weight of the knowledge is like a sledgehammer bashing through her skull. She stumbles over rock and ice, back over Falls Avenue, trying to outrun her skin, to outrun feeling. She goes into the house, hushed in sorrow, and into her room, not bothering to remove her boots and winter clothes until the door is closed. She scrambles desperately now, pulling off her clothes, opening the grate to seek out her writing book and pen, her hands delving a second time into the space to surface with a bottle of tooth polish and two stray matches. She chews the tops off the matches, swallowing them, and drinks the remainder of the tooth polish. She throws the empty bottle and the frayed matchsticks down into the hole, replaces the grate, opens her black book, and begins to write.

ঽঽঽ

I am taking my secret book and in my mind I am leaving this house where we lived. This house that echoes with your hearty laughter, tormenting me because I know I will never hear you laugh again. All I have are my words, words I wish could reach into another world, wherever it is that you are. I need to tell you my secrets, to tell you the thing that is wrong with me. But I waited too long. And now I am sick with the weight of those words that I couldn't speak, sick with the weight of your being dead. I don't want to write anymore. I just want to sleep and forget about you. I want you to leave me, so I can feel lightness again. In my mind I am crossing the river in a boat and I am walking into the hills to a little camp that is meant only for me, to a bed that is warm and free from dreams. To a place without memories so that I can sleep and forget everything that ever happened to me.

ॐ

AFTER A LONG SLEEP SHE WAKES and sits cross-legged on her bed. As she stares out the window she thinks of the house and wonders how could it be that the house seems full with the loss of him? Full to spilling with the emptiness caused by his being gone. Forever. Forever gone.

She gets up and goes out into the hall. The house is dark. Quiet. The boys must be all in bed. From the living room she sees the glow of candlelight spilling out of the kitchen. Mother.

She moves toward the light, silent but for the swish-swish of her dressing gown. Mother sits in her chair, hair undone and spilling about her. In this light, her mane of lustrous brown appears not to end but to become the wool that is being transformed in her hands into a cloth of knots and twists. Her hands contort with a dancer's agility, on and on she knits, faster and faster, her rhythm hardly broken when coming to the end of a row.

Rosa sinks to her knees just outside the threshold between the dining room and the kitchen, half obscured by the wall. Tears fall down her cheeks as she watches her Mother. It must be like praying for her. Somewhere inside the mad whirl of creating a beautiful garment to be worn, pressed to the skin, is a state of grace. Perhaps, she thinks, Mother knits to keep from crying. She knits to overcome the need. Into the sweater is woven all worries, all thoughts of dear ones, flights of fancy, comfort, warmth, and love. Maybe this is how she gives up her worries to God. She knits them all away.

Rosa gets up and moves toward Mother, her knitting rhythm still unbroken. She puts her hand on Mother's shoulder and whispers;

"It's too late. The magic code. It's too late."

Mother looks up, her face full with sorrow. She places her knitting aside and pulls Rosa down to sit in her lap. Rosa curls up, wrapping her arms about Mother. She closes her eyes and when she breathes it is full of the sweetness of Mother. Mother's hair tangles about her, reminding her of what it was to be a baby; spellbound with the magic of her hair, like a soft safe forest in which it was such easy pleasure to become lost. Like a silky dream in which to plunge her pink starfish hands, fingers surfacing rich with that wealth of hair. Rich with the comfort and the knowing of it. Rich with the mother of it.

In the days before the funeral, home expands again to embrace older ones. Little ones sleep on couches and the living room floor to make beds available. The freezers quickly fill up with food. Baked meals, meat, and fish brought in abundance by neighbours, people of the community concerned for how they will afford to eat now that their breadwinner is gone.

When Rosa hears a knock on the door, she will bolt up and run into her room, starting like a fawn caught grazing. Met by the presence of any outside family, her tears will burst forth, like water over a dam and flow forcibly down her face, salt on tongue melting words, dispelling the myth of composure.

Forced to attend the wake, she stands helpless in the sickly sweet smelling centre of the room, not wanting to look at Father's painted carcass laid out in its death box, and not wanting to meet eyes with kind people who express sympathy. Unable to fulfill her duty, she wrestles her little gold ring from her finger, and places it quickly between the folds of Father's suit. Not daring to look at the face, she bids the body goodbye, turns and walks directly into the bathroom, locks the door and weeps.

At the funeral, seated amongst siblings, Rosa listens as Catherine, greatly pregnant, sings "Abide With Me". She watches with blurred vision how her sister's beautiful belly heaves under the black velvet of her dress. Even the baby knows and feels loss, Rosa remarks, closing her eyes and willing the voluptuous soprano to continue unbroken. How will we be now? She wonders. How will we be happy again? With what will I fill this hole in my gut? How now brown cow? The words Mother would ask her to repeat when learning to sing, words laden with the task of opening the sound of her vowels, sounds meant to transcend her Newfoundland accent. How now brown cow? This maddening phrase resounds in her head again and again in an effort to hold mind and body together until she can find a private place in which to fall apart. How now brown cow.

Soon there are more goodbyes, and the emptying house senses the weight of its loss. It seems the house is in mourning. The roof has begun to leak. Throughout the house there are buckets; empty salt beef, ice cream, and giblet buckets placed to catch water that drips incessantly through widening cracks in the ceiling. Bits of sodden plaster fall away, splashing as they land in buckets that mourn their inability to contain the flow.

The nuns from All Hallows convent are coming for tea. Wondering when the young ones will go back to school, Rosa supposes. She spends all morning tidying, vacuuming, and placing blankets over the couches and chairs to hide the deep holes in the cushions. These have been dug unawares by little ones who let their hands do the worrying, and now the grieving, keeping pain secret from the rest of the body.

Sitting upright, knees together, dressed in tidy clothes beside Mother and Gramma on the couch, Rosa keeps smoothing the blanket cover, fearing exposure to these Brides of God. Sister Ignatious, Sister Mary, and Sister

Elizabeth sit, two on the couch, one in the armchair, swathed in shapeless black frocks, habits, and shoes. Their sallow faces smile as they sip tea, nibble Gramma's shortbread, and voice opinions of how Father is with God in heaven now and how the glory of heaven is a better home than any on earth.

Mother, who takes little notice of much these days, remarks on the blanketed furniture, and pulling back the one beneath her, reveals the holes.

"Oh look what Rosa's done," she laughs. "She's embarrassed by the state of our furniture so she's covered it up to keep you from noticing!"

"Oh Dear One. Sweet t'ing," the sisters tut-tut, as if she were a puppy caught crapping on the floor. Rosa, embarrassed beyond words, runs from the room, and despite even her Mother's sweet entreaties, will not appear again until the sisters have gone.

There is a gaping hole where my belly used to be. Although it was my dreams that made this apparent to me, I know it to be true. In the light of day I might not look any different, but at night my real body presents itself to me in all its absences, all its deformities. Where there used to be warmth and happiness is nothing but a hole where the wind blows through and I am empty of myself, empty of goodness and life. During the day my belly feels sick and tense, twisted with dark feelings and at night the darkness eats right through the flesh, leaving me raw and open. If Mother is right, and I have yet to be convinced, that God will take all our worries away from us if only we would give them up and have faith in him, then I have nothing to give. For everything of feeling in me has vanished into the night, and although it returns in the day it is not really there to begin with. If God is really so helpful, why does he burden us with these troubles? Wouldn't a benevolent God want us to be free of all ills? Wouldn't a benevolent God who really gave two shits have spared Father from rotting away in front of our eyes? Couldn't it have been someone else who wasn't needed to look after so many, someone who was an asshole, someone who deserved it? How can I trust in a God who is intent on killing my family? Oh damn, I am so angry. I don't know how to get rid of this feeling. I don't know how to make it stop. I wish it would stop.

ॐ

NOT KNOWING HOW TO FILL THE SPACE Father
has left, Rosa barks orders at her brothers.

"Stomp the snow from your boots would'jye, ye
bunch of meatheads, you're gettin' the floor all wet," and
"Hang up your clothes, you bunch of turkeys, for God
sake, what's wrong with you?" and many more. Orders
made to order, to outfit the size of crime on any occasion.
Orders that if adhered to might bring a kind of sense and
meaning to this meaningless time.

The brothers draw tight boy-only circles around
themselves. No longer welcome in the society of wood
adventurers, Rosa stands on the outside, helpless to
penetrate new games, new trails, new camps, new
language understood by boys only. Her attempts to
translate, to decode, catch in her throat. Garbled,
hawked gobs spew forth invective phrases. She is
incapable of treating or even naming this plague inside

her. She spends hours locked inside her room. Quarantine.

In these secluded hours she begins to write the story of Father. Just for her, just to remember before time makes her forget the smells, the sound, the closeness of the only man good enough, safe enough to touch. Stories. What is unknown must be made up. Told to the self until the story becomes truth and truth becomes memory.

She travels back in time before there were children. Back to a time seen captured in pictures. A young man. Dark. Lean. Muscled. He wears shades against the sun browning his skin on Manuel's beach. Even then the wry smile. The smile bent from hours spent at tedious work.

They were young when they married, as most were then, she supposes. In the beginning, Father had to quit school to find work to support a wife and the first of many children on the way. What did he really want to be?

He began by selling washers and dryers for an outfit that became Sears. His territory was across the water in the Bay of Islands, in the communities of Irishtown, Summerside, and Meadows. He left his boat tied up at Riverside Drive where he'd bring the company truck with the washers and dryers in the back. Each one he'd load onto his bright orange with green trimmed dory and row across the bay.

At the far shore he'd tie up the boat, hoist the cumbersome appliance onto his back and hike up over the shrub speckled cliff, going door to door, carrying it on his back.

And they would buy. Women working at home, signing to pay over months and years what would ease sore backs and soften calloused hands too soon aged from the muck of a hard earned living. Who could say no? She imagines what these women beheld when the door opened. More than handsome, heartily built to last, with that space in his front teeth that gave a brazen depth to his smile. Charming, they must of thought.

Oh, she envies time. What she would give to own that time. To have it locked in her heart and body. To not need her mind to conjure what time has taken away. How did he feel when the sun beat down, the rain pelted, or the wind whipped him on those journeys across the bay? Did he think fondly of his children at home who were depending on him? Did he curse his lot? Wish to be free from the constraints of family? Were his sleeves rolled up and his jacket folded on the seat behind to keep it from wrinkling? Did his hands weep when the blisters burst? Did it sting when the salt swam inside? What did he think about on those days in that time?

These and many more questions she scribbles furiously, tears blotting the words, staining the secret pages. Who could answer these questions now that the body was burned and the soul . . . ? Where is his soul? Where did his being go? To heaven? Father was no real believer in the Catholic God, even though near the end he'd attend mass to please Mother. He always sat at the back, never making the pilgrimage to the altar for Holy Communion. Who now could be asked to explain why only men were holy enough to become priests? Why there was no place for girls on the altar of God? Why children were born guilty of a sin they don't remember and are too young to understand? There is no one else, Rosa feels, to answer these questions, so she never asks. She stops asking, stops engaging, and soon the family comes to accept her silence, her reproachful looks for the way she is.

Gramma worries more than ever these days. While she worries she bakes cookies and hides them in tins under her bed. She thinks this is her secret. Rosa has seen tins upon tins of chocolate chip cookies growing stale in rows in Gramma's little room. Gramma has to serve the after school meals as Mother works now at two jobs. To make ends meet, they call it. To what end? This too-often repeated phrase worries Rosa. There hasn't been a walk with Mother in a very long time, she can hardly remember when the last one had been. It is as if everyone in the house is living in separate lands; opening doors onto a common shore where they wash, eat, grunt at one another, then retreat, each to their own. Mother works all the time, coming home to prepare great pots of food for the next day. She never plays the piano, and has stopped singing along with the operas on CBC radio, Sunday afternoons.

Instead of reaching out as she wishes she could to be cuddled and small and safe again, Rosa retreats in the company of silent anger. Anger for everything changing, anger at God for having let Father die. Anger she wraps around her like a cloak. Pressed to the skin. Barrier to the cold. Shield against love.

One afternoon while standing in the living room screaming at the boys for the usual reasons, Rosa hears her voice as if from afar. Bitter words. Harangued vocal cords. She stops, drops the broom and dust pan in the middle of the floor, and walks out of the house. Her stomach heaves in disgust at her acid tongue. Rosa walks deliberately, stretching her legs to their maximum stride, crossing the highway at the entrance to Steady Brook, then up the old road where in summer fireweed sprouts between cracks in the asphalt. Up the trail on the mountainside, the air thick with the scent of spruce. Over the rocks past the falls, through the high water and round the bend clinging to huge granite rocks that lead to the first swimming hole. Rosa lies, her back pressed to the cold of the only flat rock, and closes her eyes, looking inside for a reason to feel good again. At one time, the sound of water rushing over rock could always bring her peace. Now even the water can't fill the gaping hole in her gut that nags at her, demanding filling.

She springs up and begins clawing at her clothes, shedding pieces in an incoherent fashion. A rubber boot, a sleeve, a sock. Scrambling naked, on hands and knees over the rocks, into the swimming hole rimmed with ice she slides. Seal style. Belly and feet. Into the black water where there is no sound, no sight. A scream pierces the air, ripping through the heart of quiet. Rosa emerges, violent with shivering, lips and nipples blue. She pulls on her clothes, tugging at the places where they stick to her wet skin.

The light begins to fade. Running to reach the road while water can still be discerned from rock, she falls time and time again into the frigid water, reopening old wounds on knees that despair they'll weep eternal. When she reaches the falls, and stands on the great slab of marble that hangs over, she leans toward the edge and peers into the mist below. Braided hair falls across her pale freckled cheeks as she wonders at the power of her compulsion to jump. Rosa jerks back, afraid of her desires, and scrambles up the mountain path then down again as it descends to meet the old road. Her way home is lit by a gibbous moon. She runs full out, her socks squishing against the walls of her rubber boots.

Back on Falls Avenue, panting for breath, she sees her family in the kitchen through the trees. Rosa stands in the garden, black against the sky, watching their mouths move without sound. Moving through the places where Father should be. She squints her eyes, hoping to see a blur, a hint of him. Hoping he is still here, only unseen, unheard, watching everything. There is nothing of him to see. He is gone.

Her response to this fact is an acute pain in her belly. Glutton for more, she turns now to the entrance to the trail. In the trail the trees are whispering to one another. They confer within each family, birches to birch, spruce to spruce. Rosa passes them by, nodding her head to let them know she is aware of their talking. Deeper into the trail she goes, following the path until it bends at the base of the old oak tree. Knowing what she must do, she lies down in front of the tree, body on the root ribbed earth, moist with leaf rot, musty with decay, and places her cheek against the tree. She closes her eyes. After a time the memory comes to her full and head on, like a car crash. The degrading scene that took place on these very roots plays through, this time her mind's eye is relentless, it must see what happened afterwards.

It was a few months later that the bleeding began. Not at the expected time but much sooner, and a little more each day, coming with cramps that were not the usual ones, the ones that had started shortly after her eleventh birthday and were supposed to make her feel like a woman. These cramps were early and more sinister and she knew they couldn't be talked about. She had to hide them, ignore them, and for a few days she did. And then one night, the cramps became so severe they woke her up and when she went to the bathroom and sat on the toilet she heard a small "plop". And now her mind's eye sees what it was floating slowly down in the red toilet water. And before the flush sucked it away she saw it. The tiny head, the limbs beginning to distinguish themselves, a hint of their possibility, its body so small, curled in on itself like a fiddlehead, like the ones that grew in the back garden under the shade of the big maple trees. They grew for a few precious weeks before unfurling into wide feathery ferns, as they were meant to.

Now she knows she cannot live alone with this secret. She must tell him what happened. Before her eyes are open she can smell him, smell his particular skin scent beyond the smoke from his cigarette. When she sees him she stifles a scream. He is not Father of the dimpled cheek and tall story, Father stronger than all the world. He is as he was before death, as he was slipping away for all those painful weeks. Face sunken in, skin translucent, eyes dim and haunted. And there is that smell. A smell that until now had been shut away in that drawer in her memory, the unbearable one. That smell must be the scent of death. The scent of rotted flesh, and underneath just a sliver of breath. Breath fouled by illness. She recoils from him, immediately regretting having shown him so obviously what she feels. He sits on the moist ground, his legs shrunken and wiry, drawn up, his back caving around them. He draws long on his cigarette.

"What is it my girl that you have come so far to tell me?" he asks her in a reedy voice. Rosa opens her mouth to speak, but cannot make a sound. With her mind she wills her voice to carry the words to him. Just to say it out loud. Just once. To confess.

The feeling of telling is like surfacing from deep under water and filling the lungs with a first full breath of precious air. She takes a deep breath and another and another, revelling in the ease and joy of it. And when she looks back toward Father, he is gone. Only a wisp of smoke remains.

ॐ

"ROSA? I'VE FOUND HER! ROSA? ANGUS, GO TELL
MOM SHE'S IN THE TRAIL!" Seamus approaches.
He places his hand on the small of her back. She
doesn't respond. He turns her over.

"Holy crap," he groans, seeing her face, skin etched
with deep creases from the various layers of birchbark.
He takes her by the arms, stumbling as he struggles to
help her stand. Angus, followed by Jacob and Mother,
run into the trail, their way lit by the flashlight Mother
holds out in front of her like a magic wand.

"What's wrong with her? Is she all right?" demands
Mother.

"Yeah, I think she just fell asleep," Seamus answers,
patting his hand on her back.

"I wasn't sleeping," she protests, "I was just lying
here." Mother places her hand on Rosa's head.

"Oh, my darling, what's happened to you? Bring her into the house, Seamus." They file out of the trail, across the road, and into the house where Gramma awaits, holding the door open for them.

"My goodness gracious, what's happened?"

"She's fine, Mom, make her a cup of tea, would you? Angus, go rinse a face cloth with warm water and bring it here please."

Rosa lies down on Mother's bed. When Angus returns with the cloth Mother begins to wash Rosa's face. Gramma bustles in with the cup of tea. Rosa opens her eyes.

"Rosa, what are you doin lyin' around in the woods 'bye?" Seamus demands.

"Yah," says Angus, "You had Mom and Gramma cryin not knowin where you were."

"That's enough, boys. Please go on to bed now and let Rosa rest." Mother ushers them out of the room, then she and Gramma sit on either side of the bed. Rosa sips the tea.

"Rosa, tell me what happened," pleads Mother.

"Nothing happened. I went for a swim at the Falls. Then I came home and just wanted to take a walk in the trail. I lay down to take a rest by the big tree. That's all."

Mother regards her silently. Gramma shakes her head and begins praying the rosary, barely audible under her breath. Her white wrinkled fingers rub the wooden beads clasped in her palm.

Mother goes to her dresser and opens the bottom drawer. She withdraws one of the tins, places it on her bed, then fetches from the lady sculpture a key kept in the bowl at the base. She returns to the bed and unlocks the box.

"There is something I've been meaning to give to you," she says as she places a little broach in Rosa's palm. It is made of coloured glass pieces shaping swirls and flowers, four of each placed alternately in an oval shape around a centrepiece of a pink rose, all set in bronze.

"It's beautiful," Rosa whispers, turning it over to view the back. There, one tiny word is engraved. Italy. A new place for the list.

"Your Father gave this to me years ago," Mother speaks softly. "He was walking along the beach in Cow Head one day and kicked it over in the sand. He cleaned it and gave it to me. It's Venetian glass, very fine. It comes from the city of Venice in Italy."

"How did it get to Cow Head beach?"

"No idea," smiles Mother, her eyes twinkling like jewels held up to the light. "It's for you to keep. To remind you of the world out there and of your family here. We must all remember each other. We must ask God to keep love for one another in our hearts. We must ask God to take care of Father and allow him to watch over us. He will be our guardian angel. He will take care of us all."

Rosa looks at her Mother's beautiful face. She wants to believe.

"Do you think he still exists somewhere?" she asks.

"Of course I do. He exists in our hearts and minds. Every time we remember him he exists. As long as we keep loving him he will be alive in us."

Mother holds her for a long time, humming softly, rocking back and forth. Eventually Rosa disentangles herself from her mother's arms and walks through the dark house to the bathroom. Still in the dark, she begins to draw a bath. She sits on the edge feeling the steam rise to caress her face. She slips out of her clothes and steps into the bath, sucking in her breath in response to the heat of the water. Sliding down under the surface, until just her nose remains above, she takes deep slow breaths, her belly rising out of the water and sinking again below. Denying her senses like this, she is only aware of her belly, and its isolation from the rest of her body. She places her hand on its smooth flat surface and remains like that until the water loses its heat, her hand rising and falling with her breath.

This night she does not wake, she does not dream. She sleeps long and deep and when she wakes in her own bed she hears birds singing in the Scotch pine in the front beyond the window. Their song so sweet makes her think of berries bursting.

॰

"I ONE THE GEARBOX." Jacob offers as a beginning, as an excuse to enter her room and sit down on the bed.

"I two the gearbox." She smiles.
"I three the gearbox."
"I four the gearbox." The pace quickens now.
"I five the gearbox."
"I six the gearbox."
"I seven the gearbox."
"I ate the gearbox." Rosa says with a smile. Jacob bites his tongue with glee, and shaking his fist in the air, celebrates his victory.

There are these family games, nonsensical games, games so old their origins are unknown. They lurk just out of sight until some spark of memory, or flash of madness lands them full force in the centre of an afternoon, when the sun slanting through the window at just such an angle makes carrying on seem like exactly the right thing to be doing. And so in their own particular family way they play.

"I knew a girl from Port-Aux-Basques."

"Yah. S-S-She had pimples on her ass." And loud laughter.

"I knew a girl from New York City."

"Yup. 'Cause s-s-she had pimples on her titty." And she must promise not to tell Mother. She promises. Jacob begins again,

"I asked my mother for fifty cents to see the elephant jump the fence," he pauses, entreating her to join in. They both chant, the rhythm and volume increasing until they are almost shouting. "He jumped so high he touched the sky and never came back 'till the end of July. I asked my mother for fifty more to see the elephant sweep the floor, he swept so fast he broke the glass and all the glass went up his — " and they burst into laughter instead of saying the word.

One by one the other boys find their way into the room for a visit. First Angus, then Seamus, and finally Andrew, who climbs up onto the bed and bounces happily as they chat.

"I one the dingbat," Jacob begins again.

"I two the dingbat," Seamus picks up the game.

"I three the dingbat," says Angus. And the game goes round the circle until coming to an end with Rosa having to eat the dingbat.

"So me and Angus were talking about building a camp in the back of the garden, over behind the fire pit," Seamus offers to further the conversation.

"Oh yeah? Where will you get the wood?"

"Donny Gosse said his Father'd give us all the scrap he's got from when he tore down his old shed last summer," Angus tell her. "We thought it would be good to start next weekend so it'd be ready by the beginning of the summer."

"Who's all in on it?" Rosa asks, wanting an invitation to join in this creative folly.

"Me and Angus and Jake and a few of the byes, but you can be in it too as long as you don't go acting like you're the queen of it all." Seamus smirks.

"Shut up, you turkey," she retorts. "Of course, I want to be in on it."

"Yeah, me too," pronounces Jacob emphatically.

"I said you, didn't I?" Seamus gives Jake a shove toward the wall.

A silence falls, the air heavy with the awkwardness of being without him. Father's absence exists in the room like a huge hole they must jump over for their words to be audible to one another. They play at this game, growing weary from the effort of propelling themselves up and over the pit. They rest for a time, each in safety at their own place around this absence. Out of the silence, Andrew speaks ever so clearly, his words descending into the void and filling it up.

"Fadder," he says in his sweet little boy's voice, "he's gone to heaven. He's up in the sky with the wind. Mudder tole me dat. It's true. Flying in the sky, like the wind," he says sweetly, his hands fluttering above him to show them how Father is now. He looks into the eyes of his brothers and sister.

"It's true," he repeats to each of them. And they smile. They smile at one another as the idea plants itself in each of their imaginations. Yes. Flying with the wind.

ৡৡৡ

Something new is happening to me. Though I still wake at night I am no longer filled with anxiety. Though I dream, my dreams are no longer filled with fear. I told him. And I think he must have really have heard me because I feel at peace. And for the first time since all this happened I feel good. Just simple. I want to feel good. I will no longer eat things to make me sick. I know it. I am so thankful for this feeling. I was really tormented before. Tormented because I thought it was my own fault for that terrible thing having happened to me. So I found a thousand little ways to punish myself, all of them adding up to my unhappiness. And then Father got sick and everything fell apart. I cannot believe in the rite of confession to a priest, so I sought to make my own penance. And that was stupid and sad. I no longer think it was my fault. I think bad things just happen, and not necessarily to those who deserve them. It's all a part of living. I have to think of Father's dying this way, too. Maybe he

Tara Manuel

could have prevented it if he'd quit smoking years ago, but who's to say. He still didn't deserve to die. But it was him that died, not us, not me. And that didn't happen for any reason I can discover. It just happened.

All my feelings about God and the church are so mixed up in this, feelings like a turmoil rather that clear thoughts. I don't know what to believe. We must all make our own peace with this world, with this living. I believe that. Mother believes in the Catholic church and its teachings. That is her truth and I respect it. But I must seek my own truth and cannot accept simply what I am told. Mother is as right in her thinking and her believing as I am in mine. And I love her for it. I will try to follow her in offering my worries up to God. In this I must believe, because I can't hold on to them and be happy. And I just want to be happy. When I know how, I will make an offering.

I dreamed a wonderful dream tonight and though it caused me to wake in the dark, I was not grieved. In this dream I was walking up into the mountains on the other side of the river. It was day and the sun shone through the trees, the leaves and needles casting a million fertile shadows on the ground. I watched the shadows fall across my boots as I hiked up and over the hills, finally coming to the edge of the pond where Father had taught me to fish all that time ago. I sat down on a rock and it seemed ages I was there, just marveling at how the sun made the water appear so blue. So blue that it could have been the clear night sky I watched. That's when I saw it. The great Albino moose. He didn't seem to emerge from the woods beyond, but rather to simply appear in the water, drinking heartily. He took no notice of me, but continued to drink. Then, as clear as a bell, I heard these words as if he had said them aloud:

"The woods are alive with memory and passions that extend back into time before men and women and little girls. I tell you this not to make you fear the woods. I tell you this so you will respect them."

And then he was gone, just in the same fashion in which he'd appeared. Suddenly. And I am left to wonder whether this was Father coming to me in a dream, or whether simply the result of my own fancy. Whatever it was, it causes me to smile.

ॐ

ONCE AGAIN IN THE MIDDLE OF THE NIGHT, Rosa discovers her Mother by candlelight, knitting in the kitchen. This time she does not spy, but rather enters the room and sits without awaiting an invitation.

"Why aren't you in bed?" asks Mother.

"Can't sleep. You?"

"Same." And they smile at one another. Rosa sits in Father's chair, crossing her legs beneath her. Mother continues with her knitting. It is the same fisherman knit sweater she works, knit in a lovely fir green.

"Who's going to wear it now?" Rosa asks.

"I thought I would wear it. It'll be big, but I don't mind."

"It's going to be beautiful," Rosa assures her. "There's something I've wondered about for a long time." She hesitates.

"What's that my darling?"

"Why did Father set fire to the ski-do?"

Mother makes a noise between a laugh and a groan, her eyes roll back, and it seems for a moment that she is far away.

"Why didn't you ask him that yourself?" She stops knitting and watches Rosa.

"I used to ask him, but he never would answer me. So I stopped and then after he became sick I guess I was afraid to ask him."

"Sometimes your Father did things without knowing why he did them. With the ski-do . . . Well, I think what happened was he was burning leaves in the garden, he used to do that every year instead of having to rake them all up, the fire got a little out of his control and came too close to the ski-do. And then he just let it happen. Rather than try and salvage it he just gave up and let it burn. He just gave up." Mother puts her face into her hands and begins to cry. Rosa goes to her and wraps her arms around her.

"I'm sorry," she says, "I didn't mean to upset you. I didn't mean to make you cry."

"It's all right. It's all right. "Mother says, wiping her eyes, "it was just his way. When he felt something was out of his control, he just gave up fighting. I think he believed in fate. Like when he got sick, it was as if he felt there was no point in fighting for his life. No point in quitting smoking. He believed he'd die from it anyway. He believed that it was meant to be. And something in him refused to interfere with what he felt was fate. So I guess he thought there was no point in bothering himself to salvage the ski-doo if it was going to be damaged anyway."

They both sit back in their chairs and watch the fire. Mother picks up her needles and wool. Rosa looks up at her.

"Maybe you could teach me to knit!" she says, surprised to hear the words coming from her mouth. And now that she has said them it makes perfect sense that she should learn to knit.

"Here," says Mother, reaching into her knitting bag beside the chair and pulling out a pair of needles. She hands them to Rosa and reaches to the floor, picking up a small sample of the green wool she is using to knit the sweater.

"Use this for now. Just to learn the technique."

Mother moves her chair closer to Rosa's, takes the needles and wool from her and shows her how to cast on. She makes five stitches then unravels them and hands them back.

"Now you try." And slowly, with Mother's coaching, she makes a number of stitches. Mother shows her the garter stitch.

"Right needle under and through, wool under and over, pull it through and off the needle. That's right. Now you can knit anything; clothing, a fence, a tent, a camp even!" They both smile at this idea.

Morning finds the two knitters sitting side-by-side, Mother watching the changing light without ceasing her work. Rosa watches Mother's hands, able to continue working those complicated stitches while her eyes drink in the morning, while her mind finds a pleasant place to rest, and she hopes that one day she will learn to do the same.

ॐ

WHEN I AWOKE THIS MORNING, the sun shone in through the space between the curtains. I opened my eyes and the first thing I thought of was eating. I thought of brown bread in the kitchen, hot with molasses, and a big mug of tea. I thought of walking hand-in-hand with my Mother through the trails, asking her to tell to me the names of the wildflowers, thinking I will begin a list of them, and felt joy that spring is finally here and soon the flowers will be out. I then realized that I had slept through the night. I had a dream, but it didn't wake me up. I dreamt that I was flying. I was flying over the Humber Valley, collecting all the things that are precious to me and putting them in my belly. I scooped up a handful of black water from the river, I tore a thin strip of curly bark from a birch, several fingers of needles rich with perfume from a spruce, stones from the mountain streaked through with flesh coloured marble, and some soil from the garden red with life. I flew around our house, looking in each of the bedroom windows to watch my sleeping family. My heart swelled with love and I put that in my belly to seal the hole. All these things will keep me together. And love will live inside me.

Workmen are coming to begin fixing the roof. The air is rich with spring, there will be a warm breeze off the river, and I'll have to run to catch the bus. There is hope now. Hope in the morning after a full night's sleep. Hope in the air that the earth will renew itself. Hope that I am able to give up my worries. Hope in the fun of this summer as the walls go up in our new camp. Hope that I am a part of all of this living and that all of this living is a part of me. I must believe.

℘

IT IS SUNDAY. The Sunday before Easter and after mass they have planned to take a drive down around the Bay of Islands and have a picnic in Lark Harbor Park. Rosa begins her preparations. She lifts the grate and pulls out her black book. One by one she tears from the binding the pages of her writings and makes a pile of them on the floor. She takes a pen, and on a blank page writes the following:

My name is Rosa. I keep secrets. A thousand times I have imagined my Father setting fire to the ski-do. It is late and dark and he comes out from under the house with a red tank of gasoline, the kind he used for the motor boat. He goes to the back of the garden where the ski-do is parked and douses it with the gas, then steps back, lights a cigarette, and throws the match. Flames leap up, tall and fierce, they almost lick him but he doesn't move. He stands still and the fire blazes and I watch his face that is all lit up as he stares into the fire like he is trying to see. I want to know what he's looking for. I now know that's not how it happened but it's what I've had in my mind for a long time. I think sometimes he must have felt helpless. But he wouldn't tell me about it. He kept secrets, too.

They say he's with God in heaven now but I don't know where that is. If God is real then I don't think he's a man or a woman. I think God is in the mountains and the rivers, the trees and the flowers and all the beautiful things. I think God is in the feelings for what I love. I know what I love. I love my family. I love my home, even with the cracks in the ceiling and the dust in the corners. I love the river and the valley and the woods and the mountains. I love the bay and the islands and the salt water and the fresh. I love to be alive and young with everything in front of me. That's why I'm offering these pages up. To have everything in front of me. Here God in the salt water, God in the sun, God in the shore and the tides. Here are all my worries, all my pains, all the thoughts of my young girl's life. I offer them all to you. Please accept and take them away so that I may begin living anew. In this I must believe. In this I must put my faith.

Rosa places the new page on top of the pile, rolls it up tightly, and secures it with a rubber band. She squeezes the roll inside a wine bottle, making sure to force the cork tightly below the lip of the glass. She puts the bottle into her knapsack and begins to dress.

When they reach the bay road the sun radiates over the water, glinting like sparks off the tops of the islands.

The road winds up and down, curving so that the perspective of where they are in relation to the islands alters. One moment a hand could extend, and almost touch the stunted tuckamore atop of Wee Ball, the next moment the island appears a thousand miles away, an untouchable fortress blocking the mouth of the bay. To the left, the Blow-Me-Down Mountains blaze red against the sky. In the same way the mountains seem to shift close and far away. They pass through the communities of Frenchman's Cove and York Harbor, through a narrow road between two steep hills, and turn into the entrance of the park.

When they reach the beach they spread blankets over the stones; rounded and smooth, they display a plethora of origins and colours. The beach is empty but for the terns that make their nests on the shore. Rosa sits with her Mother and Grandmother, watching the formidable fishing technique of these exquisite birds. They dart to and fro a meter or two above the surface, letting out cries like the music of the piccolo, diving down into the water to rise a split second later with a fish, and take once again to the air. Their remarkable lines are as articulate as a Japanese painting.

The air smells of seaweed and salt, of life and decay. Rosa walks by herself until finding a quiet place on the shore around the point. She opens her knapsack, removes the bottle, and casts it out into the water. The wind begins to blow. Stronger and stronger, it whips her hair wildly about her head. She stands still, spreads out her arms, and invites it in. The wind finds a resting place in her belly. A shelter. A camp. She hears the wind laugh. Father lives. She smiles and runs to join her brothers who ascend the mountain trail towards Lark Harbor head, pushing one another out of the way, racing by any means necessary to be the first to reach the top.